Possession

Kane was really giving it to Mike. He busted up Mike's handsome face, using just his fist.

"You see this nigga Ace? This is what we do to those who try to get over on us."

Ace was Kane's partner and also bodyguard.

"Now I'm gonna ask you one last time. WHERE IS MY DAMN MONEY?"

Mike could barely respond. Spitting blood from his mouth, along with a few teeth.

"I spent it on beer, whiskey, gambling and a few whores."

Kane swung again.

"I'm going to make you suffer and then I'm going to kill you!"

Kane pulled out a Glock 9MM and stuck it right into Mike's bloody mouth.

"Now what was it that you spent my money on muthafucka?"

Mike was trying to say something, but couldn't, since the gun was stuck in his mouth. Kane pulled it out.

"All right man. Please don't shoot me! I have your money and can take you to get it right now."

He put the gun to Mike's temple.

"You better not be bullshitting me! I don't like bullshitters and those who waste my time, because time is something that I cannot get back."

"I'm not man, I swear!"

"Get up bastard and take me to get my money."

They got up and walked over to get in Mike's car. Kane got in the front seat, while Ace got in the back. Mike drove nervously and with full of fear. He looked out the window at the long dark road, as he drove cautiously along the way. He thought about what his wife would say, once they arrived. He knew that she would be curious of the two men with him, because she knew all of his friends, but have never seen these two before. He didn't care if something was to happen to him, but he didn't want anything to happen to her. He really adored and admired her. She was his everything and knew that she did not deserve to be caught up in his madness. He had a feeling that the night was just getting started and would linger on even longer.

When they arrived, the blinds were open and you could see his wife already setting up the table for dinner.

"Now once we get in here, I don't want no funny business, or I will kill your wife with no hesitation," said Kane.

They each got out and went inside.

Mike opened the door.

"Baby I'm home."

"Okay, love. I'm just setting up the table for dinner. It should be done in a few."

"Also, I invited a couple of old high school friends for dinner. I hope that's all right."

She came out from the kitchen and in to the living room where they were.

"Hi there! I'm JoAnn. Do you boys eat baked pork chops, mashed potatoes and gravy, with string beans? There's plenty to go around."

She was standing there with all that good body of hers. Childbearing hips, and big ass and beautiful long legs that seemed to go on forever. She had a gentle smile that brought out the warmth in the place. Her eyes were full of peace. You could tell that she had seen some things, but found a way to get towards the light. Kane was hooked.

"How could a man such as Mike get so lucky," he thought.

Kane looked over at Ace, then back at JoAnn.

"Sure we do. I'm Kane and this is my partner Ace," he said.

"All right. You boys go get yourselves cleaned up and come back in the kitchen and have a seat. You can give me your coats and I'll hang them on the coat rack. Also, take off your shoes."

They went and got cleaned up and came back to a table set for four.

"What would you boys like to drink with your chops? We have wine, whiskey, beer, water, tea, milk and juice."

"Wine is fine," said Kane.

"I'll take a beer baby," said Mike.

She got them the wine and beer.

"So how long have you've all known Mike? I've never seen you all before and I'm pretty sure that I know all of his friends."

"Oh Mike and I go way back. We played high school ball growing up. Once we went off to college we went our separate ways. You know how it is. Ace here is just tagging along with me. He's my business partner."

"Oh I see. Mike here never really talk about his past life. So any time I meet someone of his past I'm intrigued."

The timer for the food went off.

(Ding)

"I guess the food is ready now. I hope you fellas have a big stomach."

She went around loading up each plate and pouring the wine, filling up their glasses.

"Bon Appétit."

They ate quietly and drank their wine, without much talking. Every now and then, JoAnn would ask how was the food and the guys would say fine. JoAnn was very good at making small talk. Mike ate slowly and was growing anxious. He began to sweat.

"Baby are you okay? You're over there sweating bullets."

"I'm all right baby," said Mike.

They finished up dinner and went out back to the garage. JoAnn had stayed behind to clean up.

"All right Mike. Your wife's cooking was scrumptious, but now let's get down to business."

He pulled out his gun and told Ace to guard the door.

"Where did you put my money?"

"Okay, listen. I don't have it on me right this second, but. . ."

"NIGGA WHAT? WHAT DO YOU MEAN? ARE YOU SAYING THAT MY MONEY ISN'T HERE?"

"Well, not exactly, but. . ."

"FUCK THAT SHIT! I want my money in the next ten seconds or I'm going to blow your fucking head off you dick eater!"

The garage door rattled. It was JoAnn. Ace looked over at Kane to see what he wanted to do.

"Let her in."

He put the gun away in his back pocket.

"I know you fellas are busy, but I was wondering if you wanted some more to drink? I brought you beers."

She handed them each a beer and they thanked her.

"So JoAnn, may I ask you a question," Kane asked.

"Sure."

"Are you happy with your marriage?"

"Why, of course! Haha that's kind of a silly question don't you think?"

"Not really. There's plenty of unhappy couples who are married. Okay next question."

Mike had the look of worry on his face. He never could hide his emotions good. So anything he felt it showed easily. He didn't know what was coming next and feared for her JoAnn's safety. Kane looked over at Mike and gave a light smirk, before putting his view back on JoAnn.

"What bout the sex? Does he fuck you good?"

JoAnn looked over at Mike nervously and uncomfortably to see if he would say anything, but he didn't. He just looked back at her. Her body language had change and she was getting curious as to what was taking place now.

"WHAT?"

Her voice began to crack.

"What made you feel comfortable with asking me that and why the hell do you want to know?"

"Oh it's not just me who would like to know. Your husband would like to know as well."

He pointed his head in the direction of Mike.

"Well, if my HUSBAND don't know whether or not if he fuck me good, then I guess there's the answer to your question you sick bastard."

"Ooh that was very cold of you."

"I don't know who you've been around, but YOU'RE FUCKING WITH THE RIGHT ONE! Mike baby, I think it's time for your friends to leave."

"You know JoAnn, I have a lot of respect for you. As a matter of fact, I have more respect for you, than your punk ass husband."

He gave the nod to Ace to block the door. JoAnn turned around and noticed.

"You see Jo. If I may call you that? I used to date a woman who was just like you. Good body, fulfilling home cooked meals, wonderful sex and had the courage of lion. I thought that we were going to be together forever. . ."

"What's the point of you telling me this?"

"Hold on. I'm getting there. I'm getting there. Anyways, before I was rudely interrupted. I thought the we was going to make it.

She had it all. She was doing everything that you're doing now. All because she said that she "love me" and how it was her way of showing me that. Until one day, I came home to the bitch fucking another man in my goddamn bed that I had just bought the day before. She didn't even let me be the one to break it in with her. Now that was something I figured was rude. I had plans of marrying her and one day have kids. That all went out the window."

"WHAT ARE YOU TRYING TO TELL ME?"

He chuckled, with Mike and Ace looking on.

"What I'm saying is that How far are you willing to go for the one you claim to love?"

"As far as my heart will let me," she responded.

"Then I'm going to test that theory."

He pulled out the gun from his back pocket. Mike jumped up and screamed.

"NO, PLEASE!"

Ace grabbed him and put him in the chokehold.

He had the gun pointed to her head.

"Now are you ready for me to test your theory? I'm going to ask you again and you better give me the truth. DOES YOUR HUSBAND FUCK YOU GOOD?"

She began to cry.

"YES, ALL RIGHT! ARE YOU SATISFIED? WHAT EXACTLY DO YOU WANT?"

"Not quite and I only want what is owed to me. The thing with life is that you can never be satisfied, because the desire to want is more powerful than the desire to appreciate what you already have."

"Please, just let her go Kane and I'll get you the money."

JoAnn was silently crying. Kane looked over at Mike smirking, while still having the gun pointed at JoAnn's head. Mike was trying to break free of Ace's grip, but couldn't. He looked at JoAnn and for the first time saw fear in those eyes, that was once peaceful. He recognized her beauty and how much he had taken advantage of her presence.

"You see Mike. A man of your caliber doesn't deserve a woman such as this. How you were able to bag this is mind-blowing to me. I should just take her for myself and make her mine."

He looked into her eyes and could see that she was afraid of him, but still didn't feel as if he had scared her enough. He needed more fear.

"Are you afraid right now Jo?"

She didn't say anything.

"I SAID, ARE YOU FUCKING AFRAID RIGHT NOW?"

She opened up her mouth and spat on him. He laughed.

"haha now why would you do that? You're way too pretty for me to mess up that gorgeous face of yours, but if you do that again I will put a bullet in Mike's head AND yours bitch! Now answer the goddamn question!"

He cocked the gun back and she started crying again.

"YES!"

"Good, because you should be. You wanna know what turns me on? Fear. Seeing and feeling the fear in others really gets me off. It's like I'm having an orgasm, without actually having to have sex."

He got closer to her and ran the gun all over her. He went down her neck with it and on to her breast. He moved them with the gun and became aroused. He got closer ti her ear and whispered something into it. She looked over at Mike, with eyes of sadness and defeat. The eyes of Mike grew and confusion had taken over his face.

"If I do this, does this settle the debt that Mike owes and will you leave us alone?"

"NO NO NO, BABY! KANE, the money is underneath that rug over there that the pool table is stationed on," said Mike.

Kane looked over, then at Ace, then back at JoAnn.

"You have my word and that is all a man has in this world."

They were leaving the room.

"Yo Ace, watch him and check to see if the money is really there. If he tries anything funny, you know what to do."

"Gotcha!"

Tears fell down Mike's long wet face. It looked as if his heart and soul had been ripped out and fed to the hyenas.

The door shut behind them and you could hear Mike screaming, while Ace was giving him blows.

"Where are we doing this?"

"That depends. Where do you and Mike usually fuck?"

"In our bedroom, DUH."

"Hey now, don't get smart with me. I guess that's where we're going."

They made their way there and Kane took a look around. The room even had a married couple's feeling to it. Photos of Mike and JoAnn hung up on the wall. Including, some motivational photos with writing on them. There was a bathroom also in there, with a His and Hers sink for each one.

"So are you ready to get this over with?"

"NOT YET! There's no need to rush. Besides, it's more fun when the mind is stimulated, before the body is penetrated. We should warm up a bit first. At least attempt to make it feel natural."

JoAnn sat there waiting to be directed on what to do.

"Do you have a bottle of wine, vodka or whiskey up here to drink? I know you all must have one up here. All married couples do."

"Yes."

She walked over to their walk-in closet and came back with a bottle of Karkov.

"Jackpot!"

Kane opened it up.

"Now we celebrate and embrace the moment, by taking two shots a piece. Let's ignite the passion and let it burn our sorrows down."

They each took two hard long swigs from the bottle.

"I've been saving this for the perfect moment and that moment has finally arrived," said Kane.

He pulled a tiny white bottle, with a black cap on there. He opened it up, then inhaled it.

"Now you go," he said.

"I don't want to," said JoAnn.

"Either you go or I give Ace the word to blow your husband's dick and head off."

She took the bottle, then took a long inhale. The rush of the drug quickly took effect on her. She became horny and silly.

Unfocused and felt like a dream, she tried to stand but fell back down.

"Are you okay?"

"I'm fine haha," she said laughing.

"I'm fine, but my husband isn't haha."

They both laughed. Kane got on the phone.

"Yeah, bring 'em up."

A knock came at the door and Kane got up to open it. It was Ace and Mike standing there.

"Come on in fellas and join the party!"

JoAnn was still laughing and had taken off her clothes. She was completely naked.

"Oh no baby. What has done to you? WHAT DID YOU DO TO MY WIFE YOU BASTARD? I GAVE YOU WHAT YOU WANTED!"

"Did he Ace? Is it all there?"

"Yeah, it's all there."

"Good. Now Mike, I'm going to show you why you mustn't play with my money."

He walked back over to JoAnn.

"FUCK YOU," screamed Mike. "GO TO HELL!"

"Oh don't worry I will and I'll be seeing you there as well. Shall we tell your wife what you've been doing to her?"

"NO PLEASE DON'T!"

"And just what have my husband been doing haha?"
"Well, your husband has been sleeping with other women."

The laughter in her stopped and she fixed her posture. The look of disappointment came. She got up and walked over towards Mike.

"YOU ASSHOLE!"

(SLAP)

"HOW COULD YOU DO THIS TO ME?"

"Baby I'm so sorry. Please forgive me."

"DON'T FUCKING TOUCH ME YOU LIAR!"

Tears fell from her face again. They both started crying. Kane got up and walked over to comfort her.

"There there now."

She cried into his chest.

"You see Mike. It's always those who doesn't deserve it that usually be the ones to get and destroy it."

"FUCK YOU!"

"No thanks," said Kane.

JoAnn stopped crying and started rubbing and kissing on Kane. She grabbed a handful of Kane's dick, as she looked over at

Mike. He bust out crying. Her soft lips and wild tongue went in and out of Kane's mouth.

"Take me right here in front of him please," she said.

"Oh I was planning to do that anyway," said Kane.

"How would you like me?"

"Turn over and arch it for me."

She did, while fixing her eyes onto Mike's eyes.

"Treat me like your slut."

Kane slid it inside and begin to give her long, deep and hard strokes. JoAnn let out loud moans that awoke the bedroom walls. She gripped the sheets of the bed. Throwing it back onto Kane, as Mike continued to look on. He was crushed.

"Slap me," she said.

(Slap)

"Choke me."

He placed his hand around her neck and squeezed.

"Yes daddy. I'm your little slut!"

"Yes you are bitch!"

He continued to stroke her. Pulling her hair, spanking her ass, biting her neck and kissing her lower back.

"I'm about to cum."

"Cum inside of me," she said.

And he did.

"WHEW! You have yourself a keeper here Mike. She saved your ass. It's always the women who save the man huh haha? I'm a man of my word, so I'm going to spare you Mike."

He went into the bathroom to clean himself up. When he came back out, Ace still had Mike by the arms.

"Let's get out of here Ace. Got the dough?"

Ace shook his head yes.

"I'll see you around JoAnn."

JoAnn said nothing. She continued to lay there silently. Ace let go of Mike and they were gone. Mike and JoAnn looked at each other, then Mike ran over to JoAnn and placed his arms around her to hold her tightly crying.

"I'm so sorry baby! This is all my fault."

JoAnn didn't respond. Her presence grew cold and she said nothing. It was as if her soul had left her and now she was empty. Something had died inside of her that night. The woman who he married was gone and never coming back.

Bloody Mary

It was the hottest Jazz spot in town. Anybody who appreciated Jazz or had rhythm was in there. Including myself and my buddy Keith.

"Man there are some fine shorties in here tonight," said Keith.

We were sitting at our table watching those who were dancing get down.

"We're sure as hell to get lucky tonight," said Keith.

I kept on drinking and observing. I wasn't thinking about "getting lucky" tonight. I just wanted to drink, hear the sounds and see the women dance. Anytime you had women, music and drinks in one area it was going to be a beautiful moment.

"GAHDAMN!" You see those two women over there dancing?"

I looked to see what two he was talking about. Sure enough, they were gorgeous. One was slim, with a wide smile and soft eyes. The other was a bit shorter than Eartha Kitt. She had an interesting face that looked as if it could break at any moment, but it fit her perfectly.

"I'm going to introduce myself to them and invite them over to join us. I'll be back," said Keith.

I sat back and watched him. He went over to the bar first and got two drinks, then went over towards them. I couldn't hear what they were actually saying, but whatever it was it must've worked, because he was coming back over wearing a huge smile.

"Well?"

"They said that they were going to come over, once they come from the bathroom. Didn't I tell ya' we were gong to get lucky tonight?"

He hit me on the shoulder with a force full of excitement.

"I want the slim one. You take the one on the shorter side. There's nothing wrong with her. I don't like her face and I just prefer the other one."

The girls came back out and was walking passed us. They both looked back and smiled.

"THOSE BITCHES!" Keith yelled.

"This is why I hate meeting women in public outings. All they do is play games and scam. GAHDAMN WHORES!"

I started laughing.

"WHAT IN THE HELL IS SO FUNNY? HELL I WANT TO LAUGH TOO."

I could tell by the look in his eyes and his body language that he was beginning to get annoyed.

"You and your experiences with women. It's always something haha."

"Man FUCK these buckets!"

"On a more serious note, have you heard about the woman or women who's been going around turning men into blood sucking vampires through her sex?"

"WHAT? REALLY?"

"Yeah man. Times are getting crazier and crazier. So maybe that was a sign for you."

"FUCK THAT! I would much rather be transformed into a vampire through sex, than be a man who doesn't get ANY sex."

I could tell that Keith wasn't listening and didn't care at all. So I switched up the conversation.

"How's the old lady and kids?"

"Oh they're all good. Draining my pockets, but they're all doing fine. Sabrina's going to start the 9th grade and Tum-Tum is going to the fifth grade this year. I don't understand any of their homework they bring home. It's as if the teachers nowadays have made it more difficult than it needs to be. When we were in school, shit wasn't that simple, but it also wasn't as complex as it is now. They're teaching these kids shit that they won't even be using in life. Like the last time Sabrina came home from school, she asked if I could help her with her math homework and I agreed. You know, thinking that it was going to be something that I took growing up. So I did it the way that they taught us in school. Just as I finished, she says to me, "That's not how they taught us daddy". She got the pencil and started working out the problem up until what she could remember. I was damn lost once she showed me. I got up, walked into the bedroom and told her mother to deal with it."

We laughed and kept on drinking and listening to the sounds of the instruments that the musicians were playing.

"Do you think those musicians get a lot of women and sex?"

"HELL YEAH!"

We got another round of drinks.

"Even if you're a bad musician, the ladies will still adore you. For the women, they all wanna be seen. They don't really care about hearing the sound," I said.

"You have a point. Listen man, I'm going to drain the lizard. I'll be back."

When Keith got up to go to the can, something strange happened. The two women from earlier walked over towards me.

"Tell your asshole of friend that if he want to get some play from us, then lose that sorry ass game of his," said the short one.

"I'll be sure to let him know," I said.

"Do y'all have any plans, once you leave from here?"

"I'm not sure yet."

"Well, if y'all don't, then maybe you two should come over and have a few drinks with us," said the tall one.

"Sounds like a plan. How 'bout I get back to you, before the night is over?"

"Sure. Here's the address just in case. Give us a ring, once you're outside and we'll let y'all in."

They walked away and left the bar.

"Yo what the hell did they want?"

"Nothing much. Just for me to tell you to drop that weak ass game of yours, then they invited us over to their place. I told them that I would back to them and she gave me the address.

"WHAT THE HELL MAN? We HAVE to go! There's nothing to think about. What fuck is wrong with you?"

"Nothing's wrong. It's just that I have this feeling in my gut and it's not a very good one."

"You better ignore that feeling man! We'll be all right. We're going or I'll go by my damn self. Your choice."

(sigh. . .)

"Ah hell man, I'll go. Besides, I gotta make sure that you don't do anything stupid."

As we were heading towards the front door about to leave, we were stopped by someone from our old days.

"Well, Well. If it isn't the two celebrities."

It was a guy name Nito.

"Why are y'all boys leaving some early?"

"What's happenin' Nito?"

"Oh you know, just had to step out for a couple of drinks."

"Oh yeah? Shit it's pretty thick in here tonight."

We each looked around the bar and observed.

"So mind telling me why y'all dipping out so early?"

"A friend invited. . ."

Then I felt Keith's elbow in my side.

"Y'all boys are sneaky as hell haha. Damn man. Can I roll with y'all?"

Keith and I looked at each other.

"If he comes, then he's getting your share not mine."

"All right," I said.

"All right Nito, let's roll."

We pulled up to the girls front door.

"So who's going to knock on the door?"

"I think that you should do it Sin, since they came up to you," said Keith.

"All right."

"Wait. We need to have a game plan. Now Nito, the tall slim one is off limits. You can get the shorter one, who I was going to give to this asshole right here."

"All good with me. I'm with whatever. Just as long as there are drinks and some tress to blow."

We got out and as soon as I was about to knock the door opened.

"Hello boys. Glad you could make it. We see that you've brought a friend along. That wasn't in the plan, but no worries though. Please, come inside."

They both had change clothes and were now earring something more revealing to show off their figure and more skin. When we got inside I observed the place. The ceilings were very high and they had long hallways that seem to go on forever. The thing that stood out to me the most was how there were no photos of them nowhere in sight, which I thought was a bit odd, since I knew women always took a lot of pictures.

"You all could just sit here in the living room, while we go into the kitchen to fix some drinks and roll some trees. We'll be right back."

The living room also had no photos of them anywhere. Just a few pieces of art paintings and skull heads.

"I don't know about this shit man," I said.

"Just be cool man. Sure they're a bit strange, but let things play out. I'm sure they're cool."

"Yeah Sin, be cool man. They're giving us free drinks, trees and if we're lucky, some pussy too. What's better than those things?"

I didn't answer. I got up and walked around. Taking notice of the details in their art paintings that hung on the walls.

"It's a beaut huh? Here's your drink."

It was the short full figured one.

"Huh? Oh yeah! Sorry, I zoned out for a bit."

"A lot of these are originals that we bought from art auctions."

"You must've paid a nifty price for it huh?"

"There's no true price on art."

"So just as y'all brought a friend, we also have a few friends along with us. Also, we never got your names."

All of a sudden, the living room was filled with women of all kind. I mean there must've been about 20 or so. Tall, short, slim thick, petite, thick, fat, short hair, long hair, curly, straight, all shades of color and races.

"I'm Keith, he's Sinclair and that's Nito."

We were in the center and they were all looking at us as if we were fresh meat and they were the wolves. I looked over at Keith and Nito. Both were so caught up in all of the beautiful legged women in front of them that they didn't even notice me looking over at them.

"Let me just be blunt. My girls and I would like to satisfy and be satisfied. So we were hoping that you could help us out with that."

"Why us?" I asked.

"Shut up Sin! Why NOT us? Don't you see? This is our calling. The universe has brought us here for a reason. Don't ruin it fool."

"If you do not wish to be apart of it, then it's perfectly fine. All we needed was two volunteers anyway, so you can just sit here. You're welcome to the bar in the kitchen and some trees. Anybody else would like to blackout and join him?"
"HELL NAH!"

(BOTH)

"Perfect! Now if you two will follow me. As for you, we have most of everything in there to drink. In case you get lonely or lost, I'm going to leave Maria here to assist you."

Maria's the name of the short one, who had a strange face. They all left and it was just Maria and I now.

"So what'll be?"

"Anything really. I'm done with this one. Just as long as it's not a Bloody Mary. Those things are shitty."

"Haha you hate those too? Fucking tomato juice."

"Hell yeah I do and I don't trust those who do enjoy them."

"You're funny. I can tell that you're obviously not like your friends."

"What makes you say that?"

"Because if you were, you'd be in there with them, instead of in here."

"I guess you could say that I'm not in the mood. If it was up to me, then I'd probably leave, but since I don't want to leave them and the fact that you have free, drinks here I am."

She smiled and handed me another glass.

"What is it?"

"Jameson and ginger ale."

We toasted, then took a sip.

"You have the softest eyes that I've ever seen in a man. What's your horoscope sign?"

"Leo," I said.

"Of course! That explains it. I can tell by your body language. Your presence is very strong and dominant."

"Is that right?"

"I'm afraid so."

"I wonder how my homies are holding up in there."

"Oh don't worry about them. They are DEFINITELY getting what they came for. Even more! They are in good hands."

The more we drank the more we both began to open up. There were lots of laughter, a few sexual comments, some intense and intimate moments and a few disagreements as well. I was starting to feel the power of the drink inside. So much that I thought I saw an image of my soul and my father who had been dead for years.

"I like you Sinclair and if we could have met in another lifetime, then maybe this could've worked."

I wasn't sure as to what prompt her to say that. She put her head down, just as she said it. I could tell that she was being serious now and whatever thought that came into her mind had taken front seat of it.

"What makes you say that?"

"Do you trust me?"

"I start everyone out with a 100% of trust, until you lose it on your own."

"Good to know."

She leaned in and kissed my neck, before planting her teeth deep within my skin.

I awoke to the slim taller one and the other women standing there.

"Where's Keith and Nito?"
"Oh no need to worry about them. Where's Maria?"

"I'm not sure."

"Your friends weren't enough and we need more firepower. Do you think you could help us out?"

"Do to be honest, I don't have the energy, plus I think I'm going to head out."

"Aww so soon? But we're just getting started."
"I'm going to pass this time around. Maybe next time."

I was about walk away to the front door, when some of the other women were blocking it.

"I don't think you understand Mr. Sinclair. I can't let you leave. As I stated earlier, we need more power. Don't worry. It'll be quick."

I looked around the room to see if there was a way out, but there wasn't. They had every entrance possible blocked, locked and ready to keep me in.

"I know you're thinking of a way out right now. I'm here to let you know that there isn't. I have watchers on every inch of this area. So even if you escape my grasp right here, you won't make it that far."

"Damn, she's right," I thought.

I thought about Keith and Nito and what might've happened to them, but fuck it. I had to get myself free first and then see about them.

"Get 'em!"

They all came charging at me. I grabbed a couple bottles of whiskey and started throwing it at them. It did nothing. If this was going to be it, then I had to go in fashion. So I took one of the bottles and opened it to take a long swig. As they were closing in on me I took another long hit and as soon as one of them grabbed my shoulders, I was back out in front of the club parking lot. I had no idea how it happened or what was the cause of it, but I sure as hell was lucky. I was too shaken up by what had just happened, so I decided to walk home instead. The walk was long, but the fresh air was much needed. When I made inside of my apartment, I walked straight into the bathroom and threw up in the toilet. I flushed, then took a shit and flushed again. Looking into the mirror, I noticed how red and saggy my eyes were. My cheekbones seem to have stood out more, making my face more and more define. I didn't look like my normal self at all. I had a strange feeling in my gut. I tried to put my mind to work and remember what all happened, but I couldn't. I went and got in the bed, then passed out.

I was awaken the next day, with Maria sitting on the edge of my bed or what looked like a figure of her.

"Don't be afraid. I know you're probably shitting bricks right now and I'm going to explain it all to you don't worry. First, I would like to thank you for freeing me. You have no idea how long I've been waiting for someone to come and free my soul and as a favor in return, I've planted my spirit inside of you when I bit your neck last night."

I touched myself on the neck and instantly remembered.

"Even though you're not pure Sinclair, you are a genuine soul and that is what really makes a human special. It's not always about how pure your heart is or what you do for others. Now what I have done to you is simply given you a longer life. A long one at that. Basically, you are a vampire."

My face dropped. She grabbed me by the thigh and I could feel the coldest from her hand. She fixed her eyes on me, waiting for me to respond.

"I'm a bit mad. My emotions are all over the place. Considering the fact that I don't want to live forever."

"You don't have to. You could always go back to Lena, whenever you're ready to change back. Though, there is a chance that you might die in the process. However, I don't think she will do it, since I am her daughter."

My head dropped again and suddenly I could feel my heart sink into my stomach.

"Hey don't worry. It's not that bad. My soul needed rest. I saw how different you were from your friends, which is exactly how I am from my mother."

"So what do I do now?" I asked.

"Nothing. You go and live your life how you want to. Whatever that may be for you."

"What about Keith and Nito?"

"Your friends are dead Sinclair, but I'm sure you already knew that. Also, no one is going to remember they even existed, because once you are killed by one of us, the existences, experiences and scent is wiped away."

"Fuck!"

"I chose you. Had I not, you was going to end up like you friends and my mother would have enjoyed that. When we first saw you all at the club that night, we had already planned on getting you specifically. We knew how powerful you were, but that changed once I got to know you more. I could feel it just by being in your presence. So I wanted better for you, instead of sucking you dry and leaving you to die. I didn't want you to be just another and I also didn't want you to be forgotten."

"I mean, you still could've sucked me dry. I wouldn't have minded at all."

"Haha I see you still have a sense of humor through all of this."

"That's one thing I won't lose. Along with a few other things."

"There's three things you should know before I go."

1. You don't need to feed on humans to survive. Simply just drink red wine and you will be good.

2. Just because you are now a vampire, doesn't make you invincible. You can still be killed like every other existing thing on this damn planet. It would just take you a few times to die, before you actually are considered dead.

3. Never lose the genuine nature in you. That is what will help you remain you and control the powers that I have bit into you. If you ever lose it, then the powers will take control and overshadow you, until you are no more.

"Now I must depart. Just know that whenever you need me, look within. Until then, take care my sweet Sin."

Just like that, she was gone.

I threw on some different clothes, some shades and headed out to the bar.

Chaotic Lovers

Donnie had crooked teeth, one blue eye and one brown eye and stood about 6'0.

"I don't know how much more of this 9 to 5 bullshit I can take."

Donnie was sitting at the bar drinking a whiskey sour.

"I understood what you mean young-blood, but shit you still have a lot of time left, unlike myself. You haven't even lived long enough. If you want to have a better future, then do something worthy in your present."

I looked over at the old man whose voice was as deep as Barry White and face of a war vet, with scars and wrinkles. His hair was thinning at. the top, but his eyes were quite captivating. His hands tremor, informing me that he had Parkinson's. I motioned the bartender for another drink and bought the old-timer one too.

"Thank you, young-blood," he said.

I gave him a nod.

"We must look out for one another, whether it's physical, mental or emotional."

No matter how society ranks us. Rich, middle-class or poor. Even though it's the rich who put their foot on our necks to keep us down. Although this world is pretty fucked up and we have a shit-for-brains as our, well as the "president", there is still bits and pieces of beauty that can be found all over this world. Along with a few other hidden gems. By the way, my name is Willie Bohman, but everybody calls me Willie."

"I'm Donnie. Swell to meet you."

"SO which 9 to 5 is sucking you dry?"

"I'm a welder and though the pay is good, the job isn't. I only did it to please a woman. As time went on, I realized that she was still unsatisfied."

"I've been on this earth for six decades and have learned that people are never really satisfied. They just put a bandaid over it and keep it pushing, until it explodes again. If they want to stick around they will. If not, then they will leave. One thing you must learn is that a woman has no shame in being vulnerable, when it comes to her truth and desires."

"You're right about that."

"You only got one life. ONE! So if this 9 to 5 is really draining you as you say, then you must make a few adjustments to your life. Find your medium."

Willie finished up his drink and stood up to get himself together.

"Before I depart, I leave you with this. A fish is born with the knowledge of knowing how to swim, but does it have the understanding to know if they love something or not? When you have the answer, let me know. Until then, take care young-blood."

The old-timer was now gone. I stayed and got drunk. People came, but I didn't pay them no mind. I left the bar as they were locking the place up. I don't really remember how I made it home, but when I did Bella was already asleep. I climbed into bed with her, the fell asleep.

I awoke to Bella standing over me, with her bags packed.

"What's wrong baby?"

"I'm leaving your Donnie. All you do is drink, shun everything and fuck me whenever you feel like it. Hell you don't even go down on me. I bet if I was fucking someone else I would be getting fucked AND licked AND ate!"

Before I knew it, my hand went across that beautiful face of hers. It sent her body flying lifeless across the room and onto the floor.

"YOU BITCH! You GODDAMN SLUT! That's all you want to do anyway. You had this all planned didn't you? All of you women are the same. Once you get a guy who gives you light, some laughter, sex, shows you the art AND some spark of inspiration, you end up fucking him over. You can leave if you would like, but if you walk out that door DON'T COME BACK!"

She stood up, grabbed her things and left without looking back. I sat at home depressed. I got drunk for weeks straight and thought about Bella. Although I meant what I said when we were face to face, I still missed her presence. She was the softness that I needed, whenever this world became hard for me. I stopped going into work and didn't leave the house, unless to go pick up beer, wine, whiskey and food. I reflected on our experiences and became inspired by them. The sadness had fueled me. I had finally found my medium and out of it birthed a novel. It only took for me to lose something that was special to me and a couple of weeks of being alone. I went down to this publishing company that I found out about through a guy who worked there and had seen my work. He was already awaiting for my arrival that day.

"Well, here it is."

"Wow! That was quick. How were you able to produce such amount of work so quickly?"

"Love, drinking, depression and solitude," I said.

"I'm going to get my guys right on it! After this, you will never have to work a 9 to 5 again."

"Yeah?"

"OH YEAH!"

Me being a pessimist, I didn't believe him. No matter how much he tried to butter it up. Two weeks had gone by and I was out of a job, behind on rent and still without woman. An eviction note slid underneath my door. I tried to bring myself to care, because I didn't want to be out on the street again. At the same time, I didn't care. I figured that this was going to be the end and if I must go, then I will go out in style. I drank, wrote a couple of pieces and painted as well. The eviction said that I had until Friday to pay. The day was Wednesday.

That night, around nine pm, I got a call.

"Hello?"

"WE DID IT!"

Screamed the annoying voice on the other end of the phone.

"Who is this and what the hell are you screaming about?"

"It's Bobby and my company have now started printing copies of your book. I can't wait to see the finishing touches and have a copy of it in my hand! They said that it should be ready next week."

"That all sounds like amazing news, but listen, I'm behind on rent right now and probably won't be at this residence to receive my check from you all. . ."

"Don't you worry. I got you covered already I'll have the check over to you by 8am tomorrow morning."

"Thanks Bobby."

"No, THANK YOU! You just keep on writing. And another thing. . .Quit your job."

"Already did that."

The following week the book was out and sold like hotcakes. Bobby phoned to tell me that he had booked me for a book signing. It was going to be on that Friday, late afternoon. I went from bar to bar drinking and flirting with the women who looked just as broken as myself. Sometimes I stayed home getting drunk and hitting the keys. Letting my soul bleed out and fighting my demons. Sometimes they would win. One Thursday night, the night before my book signing, I got so drunk that I phoned Bella. It seemed as if she was asleep. I could hear her breathing through the phone. Finally, her warm soft voice spoke.

"Hello?"

"Bella it's me. Donnie."

"GO TO HELL!"

She hung up.

Friday came. I made sure that I signed every last person's book. The last book I was about to sign was this young slim body, tight face woman. She didn't look a day over 25yrs old.

"I'm surprised I made it. I was running late and didn't think you'd still be signing."

"I was just about to wrap up, but could always make an exception for you."

She blushed and smiled. Her teeth showed and revealed that she was wearing braces. They shined, once the light from the ceiling hit them. She noticed that I was looking and readjusted her face.

"Thank you for signing my book. I really love your writing! I love how vulnerable you are and how you make me feel something. It's very raw and gritty, yet so tinder."

"Would you like to have a drink with me?" I asked.

"What about your signing here?"

"Oh it'll be fine. I'm done here anyway."

"Sure."

I told Bobby farewell and went back to my place. I figured he must've gotten the idea and said that he would give me a call tomorrow. When I got to my place, I cracked open the drinks and we were deep sea diving in it. Drink after drink. The setting became so comfortable that she opened up more and begin to dance. Wild and touching herself all over, I sat there drinking and watching. She found her way to the record player and put on Badu. Her thin, but well-shaped figured swayed like the Gulf Of Mexico. We were both embracing the moment, without overthinking, as humans usually did. I heard the walls beating and thought that it was coming from the record player. So I paused it, then heard it again. The door flew open and in came Bella swinging a bat. Knocking over everything in sight.

"YOU FUCKING DOG!" THIS IS WHAT YOU DO, WHILE WE TRY TO RESOLVE OUR ISSUES?"

She continued swinging the bat in rage. Bashing dishes, putting holes in the walls, beating up my furniture, well the little I did have anyway. I tried to wait for the right moment to snatch it away from her. The bitch was swinging it like Barry Bonds. Then out of the blue she stopped. She looked over at the young sweets, (who by the way was very frighten) then charged at her with full force. Before she could get to her I tackled her to the ground.

"BITCH YOU BETTER GET OUTTA HERE, BEFORE I DRAG YOU OUTTA HERE," shouted Bella.

Hearing Bella shout that out, I feared for the young sweets. She ran out, leaving behind her belongings, with the exception of her purse and blouse. We got up and Bella went to closed the door. I got out a bottle of Jack and poured two glasses with two ice cubes in each. The night went on. It was full of rage, passion and emotional starvation. We made love three times that night. Very loud and intensely, before falling asleep.

Talking Assholes

"Do you like that orange motherfucker," she asked.

"No, but then again I don't like no motherfucker who get in that chair, since they all seem to lie about how they're going to bring change for us, when all they've really done was added more fuel to the fire and bring chaos," I said.

"I'm tired of struggling. Being poor and STILL having to fight for my life is pure hell. It's as if I'm working, just to go to work and slave. My body feels like a $2 hooker, while my mind is being a lazy slut."

We were sitting up in beed, with the lights out listening to the rain and passing the bottle back and forth.

"It's set up for everyone who isn't rich to fail."

"And that's another thing. Why must we get rich, in order to succeed and not suffer?"

I wanted to answer, but she continued.

"I just think society is full of shit and everything that comes with it."

"I agree."

"How do you feel about relationships and how they are these days? Do you think we've made any progress from the past generations? Where basically, it was only in favor of a man."

I took a long swig from the bottle. Then another. I've always enjoyed her conversations. I admire those who can think for themselves, without letting the ego get in the way and destroying them.

"Do I think we've progressed? Yes. Do we still have a long way to go? HELL YEAH!"

"Although I agree, I would like to hear your perspective on why you say that."

It's simple really. Selfishness. Men are still selfish and are afraid. The fear of a woman doing better than them would scar them for life. It's fucked up, because I always said let a woman make some changes and just maybe it'll benefit all of us. But you know, as a writer, they already think you've lost your mind. So they wait for your heart to go next, but what they don't realize is how you never lost your mind to begin with."

"I had no idea you wrote. What type of style of writing do you write?"

"And I also drink. Don't forget that haha. But I write transgressive literature and confessional poetry."

"Oh wow! That sounds like some very intense writing. I've never heard of those genres before. How would you feel about a woman becoming president?"

"Just how we were ready for a black president, we are also ready for a woman to be president. Though it won't change how I feel about the government and the system."

"I think I know what you mean by that. It's all a shitshow really."

"You have all of these people who are really puppets start out racing against each other, just for only two of them to make it. The finalists go at each other's throat. You want the puppet on the left or the puppet on the right? Choose one. The system is set up to fail. Especially, for a black man. We start off losing, as soon as we come into this world. But I won't get all into that."

I hit the bottle three times after telling her that. On the third swig I held it a bit longer. She pulled out two cigarettes and lit them both and gave one to me.

"Do you ever get lonely, crave for some form of intimacy and affection or do you enjoy being in your own solitude?"

"Honestly, I don't really get lonely. I do have my moments where my appetite for some intertwining runs wild."

"I feel the exact same way. I consider myself a nympho though. Many men say they like a woman who has a high sex-drive, until they meet one and can't even last two rounds. Hell they ass can barely go one. They all say the same tired ass shit."

(lowers her voice)

"Oh baby, let me hit you with this long dick. I got a lot of stamina."

We both laughed at how correct she was.

"They ass can never find the clitoris, which is the most important part. I've lost all faith in men, but you know, I love dick too much to wipe them off completely. So at this point I'm just enjoying the pleasure of having them be my slave and call boy whenever I need to feel something throbbing inside of me."

She kept talking, as I watched her move those lips of hers.

"Do you think there is a God or do you believe in another higher power or nothing at all?"

"I do, but I don't follow religion."

"Yeah, same goes for me. I do believe that there is a God. No matter how fucked up things are in the world."

"I don't agree with the views and perspective of different religions. Like whose really right? Maybe we're all wrong. It's very possible. What makes it even more funny is how each of them say that you shouldn't judge, yet they all still do it! A bunch of fucking hypocrites if you ask me."

"So does that mean that you believe there's a heaven and hell? If you do, which one do you see yourself going to?"

"To be frank, I'm not really sure. The more I age, the more this topic wraps it's grips around my mind."

"Hmm. . .I understand what you mean."

I could tell that she was reflecting on her life. Her face said it all.

"Oops, we're out of wine. Do you have more?"

"Yes, in the kitchen cabinet."

She got up to go get the other bottle. She was naked and when she got up those small asscheeks jumped like hopscotch. She also had a scar on the back of her thigh that I must've overlooked, because I didn't notice it before.

"It's a bit cold in here, so I turned the heater on. I hope that's okay."

"It's fine."

"Do you regret anything in life?"

It had been quite awhile since anyone's asked me that question. I didn't have a quick response. I sat in silence for a minute. I thought long and hard about everything in my life. Trying to see if there was something that I wish I could take back.

"I can't think of anything at the moment. Anyway, life will still find some other way to get what it needs outta me."

"I see. . ."

"What?"

"I gotta say, I'm quite impressed with the responses you've given me."

"Ah she underestimated."

"Not even. I just didn't think you'd give such detail answers. Do you fear death?"

"Not at all. In fact, I embrace it. Whenever I do face it. I'm going to look it right in the eyes and finally crack that smile that life's been trying to get from me."

"Well, I'll be damn! I guess you really do have a way with words."

She hit the bottle hard and a tear rolled down her face.

"What's wrong?" I asked.

She wiped her eyes.

"Nothing. It's just that I've never just sat up in bed with a man, where we both were naked, talking about life and our deepest thoughts and feelings. I mean, I'm right here laying in bed with you naked, yet I don't feel pressured by you to fuck! I really appreciate you and this so much right now. Every time I'm with a man, it's always all about sex. Don't get me wrong, sex is fucking beautiful, but shit give a bitch a break!"

I brought her closer to me and held her in my arms.

"Sorry, I hate you have to go through that."

"No, I'm the one who should be sorry. I'm over here ruining a perfectly good time by crying on your shirt. Also, your heart is beating really fast. Are you okay?"

"It's all right and yeah I'm good."

"One last question. If you had to die, how would you want to go?"

"In my sleep."

Trending news:

"Underground writer and poet Sinclair Armstrong, dies in his sleep. The cause of death is still unknown. He was found in his apartment alone."

Twitter: "#RIPSINCLAIR"

Instagram: "Damn, I was JUST talking to Sinclair."

Facebook: "Until we meet again. I love you and now you can finally rest Sinclair."

No Apples Left

It was late in the evening, on a Sunday and I had just gone to the bathroom to take a shit. Before, I was sitting at the typewriter, waiting for the magic to occur. I ate two fish sandwiches and drank a couple of beer to get the juice flowing. Still, nothing would come out. I finished doing my business in the bathroom, washed and came back out. I grabbed another beer and sat to watch the sunset. I always preferred sunsets over sunrises. It was a pleasing sight to indulge in. Once the sun set, I went back into the bathroom and ran some hot bathwater with some lavender Epsom salt. Once the tub was full, I shut off the water and got naked. I took a look at myself in the mirror. I was so damn skinny. So much that I looked sick. I begin touching myself and rub one out, then got into the hot bath. I went in with ease and slid all the way down, until the water was at my neck. Just as I was starting to get comfortable, a loud knock came at my door.

"Now who in the hell could that be?"

I got out and put on my bathrobe to walk to answer.

"My main man! I need your help, right now. So I hope I didn't catch you at a bad time, because if it is, then I'm sorry. But this cannot wait,"

It was Luchi.

"I'm sorry man, but I had nowhere else to turn to. Besides, I feel like you would understand my situation, a lot more than anyone else I would have gone to."

"It's no problem at all man. Have a seat. Would you like a beer?"

"Yeah man. The way I'm feeling right now, I will soon need something with a bit more kick to it. Shit is so fucked up this time."

I had no idea what Luchi was talking about, but I knew that he needed something that would calm him down for a second. I came back with two beers in my hand and handed him one.

"So look man, there's this woman who I've been sleeping around with for the last couple of months, without Teresa knowing. Now, the woman's pregnant and I don't know what to do."

"Wait a minute. Back up a second. Who's pregnant? Teresa or the other woman?"

"THE OTHER WOMAN! HAVE YOU NOT BEEN LISTENING? DID YOU NOT JUST HEAR WHAT I SAID?"

"I heard you I heard you. I just needed to see if that's what I really heard from your lips."

We sat in silence for a second, drinking our beers. I honestly felt bad for Luchi, because I knew how much love he had for Teresa and how much he deeply cared for her. Though, I also knew how much he fucked up. It's always those who did not appreciate it that got it. Why the rest of us who never gets it continues to suffer.

"What the hell do I do man?"

"That's some heavy shit. Personally, I don't like giving advice. Especially, on matters such as these. It's just not my thing and I feel as though the laws of nature will play you the cards you were meant to get. So no matter what I say here today, whether it works or no, life will still be the dealer."

"I DIDN'T ASK FOR NO GODDAMN LECTURE! If I wanted that I could've gone up the street, to where the bums hangout and listened to one of those drunkards."

"All right," I said. "You want some advice? Here you go. I think that you have no one to blame, but your own self. You wasn't honest with no one, including yourself and now life is repaying you. You must take ownership for the aftermath. Sure you may have a say so in it, but don't hold your breath. It's the woman's body and it'll be her choice in the end. Not yours. Yeah, you fucked up big time, but sometimes consequences after the fuck up can change your life for the better."

"Are you saying that I should tell Teresa that I cheated on her and got another woman pregnant?"

"I would. I would rather lose it all early, rather than later on in life."

"Man I just don't know what to do."
He let out a long sigh, then put his head down. I went into the kitchen to grab a bottle of Jack, along with two glasses. Each with three ice cubes in them.

"Now that's more like it," he said.

I poured us both up and we dove right in it.

"I wanna thank you for letting me come over and tell you about my shitty drama. I know how busy you are with your writing and everything. By the way, how is that coming along for you? Are your producing any good poems or stories? Is the book almost finished?"

"For a guy who has enough on his plate already, you sure do like to see what's on other people's plate haha."

We both just laughed.

"Well, I must be going. I'm going to spend some time to myself, before I go through with whatever decision I choose."

He took one last swig of his drink and really downed it, then handed the empt glass to me.

"Oh yeah, and sorry about interrupting your bath."

I walked him to the door and shut it behind him. The phone rang and I went to answer it.

"Hello?"

"Hey, are you free?"

"Who is this?"

"It's Teresa. Luchi's wife. Remember we were supposed to be meeting up, because I needed to talk to you about something? Are you still coming? It's really important."

I had totally forgotten all about that. My memory was shorter than a man who was excited about his first fuck and only lasted two minutes. I stood there contemplating for a second.

"Sure. Give me about 20 minutes."

"Sounds good. I'm at SHUCKY'S. Give me a call when you get here, so I can direct you on where I'm sitting."

"All right," I said.

SHUCKY'S was this bar that was in a lowkey area downtown. The drinks there were cheap and the restrooms had graffiti all over the walls. The music was all over the place. On certain night they had drunk karaoke, which I didn't too much care for. When I arrived, the door was open and you could see right through the joint. I got out, walked in and went straight to the bar. There was a bartender who didn't look over 21. It was a guy. Short, huge eyes and a kind face. I ordered a shot and a beer, but when I pulled out my money to pay he waved me off and pointed in the direction of a corner. In that corner was a table and a woman wearing black tight jeans, boots, a light denim jacket and her hair pulled back into a ponytail. It was Teresa. She waved me over to come.

"What's going on?"

"Hey Sinclair. First off, I would like to say thanks for coming and taking time out of your busy schedule. I really do appreciate it, which also why I paid for your first two rounds."

I could see the look in her eyes. Whatever it was must've been weighing heavy on her mind. I had an idea, but I wanted to be sure, before I made any assumptions.

"No worries, but I do thank you. So. . .What's on your mind?"

"Okay. I'm going to ask you something and I need you to be completely honest with me. No matter what or how much you think it will hurt me. Understood?"

"Understood."

What in the hell did I get myself into? First Luchi, now his wife.

"I'm just gonna come out and ask. . .Is Luchi cheating on me?"

And there it is.

"To be frank, no."

"Well, I just had to ask you, because I know y'all grew up together. So I thought you would know something, but the answer is yes. Yes, he is."

"How do you know?"

"A woman has her ways Sinclair."

"Damn."

"I know and that's not even the crazy part."

"There's more?"

"OH PLENTY!"

We each took a sip of our drink and beer. She took a long deep sigh. . ., before starting back up.

"He cheated on me with a man!"

She sat there staring in my eyes, while I sat there staring back at hers. Trying to see if she still had a soul. She did, but it sure as hell was dark. Then she started up again.

"I had been curious leading up to this, because of his actions. I was going to stalk him, but then they say, "What's done in the dark shall come to light," and so it did. He forgot his phone at home one day, as he was heading to work. I kept hearing something ring and buzz. I guess it must've fallen underneath the bed, because there is where I found it. Now I didn't answer it with the intentions of it being something bad. I know how most women do that, but I genuinely thought that it was him calling it to see where it was. So I answered and the rest was history."

She took a sip of her drink, then focused her attention back on me.

"And that's not all."

"What else is there?"

"We're going to need a shot for this one. How 'bout you go get the shots, while I go use the restroom. Don't worry. I already paid for them. "

She made her way to the restroom. I could tell that she was drunk already and didn't give a damn who saw her. I picked up the shots and went back to the table. She wasn't back yet. I had no idea what she was going to say next. I just hope that she doesn't ask for advice.

"I'M BACK!"

"Are you going to tell me now?"
"Shots first, story second."
We clanked our glasses together and threw our heads back, while the drinks did the rest.

"Ahh. That went down smoothly. You know shots are much mire easier to take when you're going through shit."

"I'm waiting," I said.

"Well. . ."

Her eyes went down towards the empty shot glass. She was no longer smiling, but had the look of someone who had lost something very dear to them.

"Luchi has a baby on the way and it's not with me."

I acted clueless to her response, even though I already knew. A part of me wanted to tell her that I had already knew, but I didn't want to cause her anymore damage, than she was already in. So I kept silent.

"DAMN!"

(It was the only word that I could mustard up)

"Damn is right."

"How did you find this out?"

"He came right out and told me today over the phone. I mean, it was the least he could do."

"This sounds like a goddamn horror story."

"It's worse than that."

"So what's next and what do you want from me?"

"You see, I know that he sees you as a brother. He has always been very fond of you Sinclair. In fact, I honestly think that he tries to go out and live his life like yours. You know him better than anyone else does. Hell maybe even better than I do. Your role in this s helping him with finding a new place to live, because I'm putting him out and serving him with divorce papers."

She took a long swig from her glass. For some reason, the oxygen in the place suddenly felt cooler. Just as her face. Not a smile in sight.

"You don't have to have an answer right at this very moment, but you will need to have one by Friday."

We left it at that and continued drinking.

Friday came, but there wasn't a knock at my door. In fact, there wasn't a knock or a phone call all day. I waited around for a bit, before I went out to go downtown to a bar. I left and got downtown quicker than usually. When I pulled inside the parking lot, I saw a car that I thought I might've recognized. I got out and walked into the bar. It was a pack house. I went up to the bar and ordered my drink. They had the TV playing on silent in the background. A guy walked up to me and I could smell the liquor on his breath.

"Say man, have you heard about that guy who went ape shit crazy and offed his mistress, wife, another man AND HIMSELF TOO! It's been all over the news all day. That's why they have the TV playing. We're waiting to see them come with more details."

I didn't respond. I just sat there and continued drinking. The news came back on and everyone was around the bar. They turned down the music and turned up the volume on the TV. I didn't pay attention to it. I just sat there drinking and watching these two guys, who also didn't give their focus towards the TV play pool.

"LOOK," one guy said.

"I hope they fry his ass in hell," another guy said.

I begin to hear clapping and chatter. I turned around to see who it was. I chugged my last beer, paid and tip the bartender and got out of there. I was so confused and had no clue on where to go. So I drove to a nearby beach and parked. I got out and walked towards the sand and sat there in silence.

"He really did it! I cannot believe that he actually did it!"

Eggshells

We were fucking so loudly that her moans had the walls shaking. I thought I heard God banging on the door, but it was our neighbor asking if we could keep it down. Instead of stopping and answering the door, we ignored it and her moans grew even louder.

"Grab my ass," she said. "Pull my hair. Choke me. Slap me. OH I'M CO-MI-NG!"

I continued stroking, until I soon came after her. I got up, went to the bathroom to get a warm washcloth and wiped her down. Her beautiful smooth skin was lovely to run my hand across. She just laid there, while I wiped her off, Her soft asscheeks just stayed put. She was more than a fuck, but not enough to be considered love. Once I got her clean, we just laid there. Passing the wine bottle back and forth. I had been living at her place for almost three months now and felt as though she would kick me out any day now. I was in between jobs at the moment and was still looking for Lady Luck to bless me by publishing one of my stories. Times were stressful, but we got by because of her mostly. There would be times where I would look into her eyes and see her disappointment in me. Humans usually did that and I was doing that to her now.

"Do you believe that you could love someone, but not want to be with them?"

She asked me the question without looking over at me. I knew then that she was speaking on me. Us. Our situation.

"Yes I do. What I don't get is why people wait so damn long to tell the person they no longer wish to be with. Love is truth, not a lie."

I could tell that she knew that I knew she was talking about us and could see the pain in those dark brown eyes of hers. The room grew silent and the only thing could be heard was our breathing.

"Maybe, it's because they are afraid of losing them and don't actually want them completely out of their life. People don't always make right decision whenever their mind is discombobulated. They usually go off of emotions."

Although I agreed with her, I still wanted her to confess her truth. People rarely did that though. She got up to go into the bathroom and shower. I watched that ass of hers and long legs sway away. She had a birthmark on her right asscheek that was shaped like the state of Florida.

"I'm going to take a shower and freshen up for work."

She closed the door behind her and I soon heard the water running. She also turned on the radio and I could hear the music, with her light voice singing along with it. I wondered what I would do today. I wanted go downtown to apply for a part time job. At least I could help out with the bills or groceries. I got up and went to the fridge to grab a beer and walked over towards the bathroom door. She had see through shower curtains, so I could see her full figure clearly. I watched the water bounce off her body with ease. The steam was rising, as she placed her head underneath the shower-head. She took the washcloth and ran in along her the curves of her body. Starting at the top with the neck, then on down to the rest of her body. I wanted to place my hand around her neck like a snake. She raised her arm up to wash underneath them. There was a little bit if hair there, but I didn't give a damn. She moved the washcloth down to her belly, where she had a pudge and I didn't give a damn about that either. She ran the cloth down between her thighs very slowly, then used her free hand to aim the shower-head down at her cunt. It was beginning to get interesting. I started to rise down in my boxers. I tilted my head back and took a long swig from my beer. She took her fingers and made them tap dance on top of her clit. Her mouth opened, teeth were shown, eyes were closed and I was jealous of the water for getting to have all the fun. She went on and on, until she finally came and quivered. I thought about going in to help bathe her, but instead I just walked away from the door. The shower water stopped and I could hear the opening of the shower curtain. I sat up in bed drinking a beer and listening to her sing softly. As I was sitting up in bed, drinking, a loud thump came against the wall. Followed by loud moans and groans. Two voices from the other side of the wall breathing heavily.

"Say you love me, you bitch!"

"OH I LOVE YOU BABY!"

"Who's your daddy?"

"YOU'RE MY DADDY BABY!"

"I GUESS THE NEIGHBORS ARE RETURNING THE FAVOR," yelled Nina from the bathroom.

"I guess so," I said.

"HOW ARE YOU FEELING?" She yelled again.

"I'm all right. I would be doing better, when one of these jobs or publishers give me a call back."

"Don't worry they will."

She came out of the bathroom with just a towel wrapped around her body and her hair still wet. She gave me a light smile to reassure that all will be well, then walked over and planted a kiss on my forehead. Her lips were warm against my skin. The loud thumping started yup again. The pictures on the wall begin to shake.

"Wow they're really getting it haha," she said.

"Does it make you jealous?" I asked.

"Only because I not getting any myself," she replied.

We both started laughing. It was good to have a woman who had a sense of humor to match mine. She was getting dress and I sat there watching her. Every now and then, she would give me a certain look and smile.

"If I didn't have to go to work in the next 30 minutes I would fuck you right this second," she said.

She was putting on her clothes. Something causal. She was an accountant for this firm downtown.

"Tell them you'll be running a few minutes late to take care of some important family business."

"Even if I told them that, with that small amount of time it STILL won't be enough. You know we can never go a short round. But don't you worry. Once I get home from work, we're eating, showering and fucking."

I continued watching her, while she finished getting dressed. She sure as hell had a nice figure to match that drive of hers.

"All right I'm off to go play superwoman. There's food in the fridge, as well as beer. I also have wine and whiskey in the kitchen cabinets, so help yourself out. Behave yourself and try not to get too drunk. Well, I probably shouldn't have said that. Knowing you, you will, just because I said not to."

She came over and gave me a kiss on the lips, then walked out of the door. She treated me so well. One of the very few who did treat me as if I needed love, instead of dog shit. At first I didn't know what I was going to do, after she left. I got up and roamed around in my boxers and looked out of the blinds into the city. I had no idea how my life was going to go and no job to avoid the anxious thoughts. I walked around that tall ceiling apartment with emptiness inside my heart and beer in my belly. I was in a space that wasn't even mine. I touched things that didn't belong to me. I felt so damn uncomfortable. I had to get out soon. I felt bad for being there in her space without a job or no incoming income. To make things easier for her, I figured that I would leave sooner rather than later. So I packed up the few bags that I did have, wrote a letter to her and placed it on top of the kitchen counter. Then I grabbed a bottle of whiskey from the cabinet and headed for the front door. I took one last look at the place and let out a deep sigh. This was a sad moment, but it was needed and I had hoped that she would understand my reasons. I shut the door behind me and place the key underneath the doormat. That was the end of that. I took a bus towards downtown to the nearest bar. When I got inside, only the bartender and a few old drunks were there. I went up to the bar and ordered a beer and a shot of vodka. The bartender looked at me and asked for my ID. I gave it to him, he looked at me, then handed it back to me. It wasn't even noon yet and here I was about to indulge in some drinking. I guess the time has never stopped me before, so why should it now? I looked over at the old timer who was sitting a few seats down from me. He looked to be drunk already and was spilling some of his drink, as he was trying to get it in his mouth. He saw me looking, then asked,

"Did you lose a woman or a job? Because either way, they both cut you deep."

"I'm not really sure about the first one and didn't have the second one to begin with," I said.

"We never do," he said. "We never do."

I finished my first round and ordered a second round.

"Give the old timer one too and yourself one as well," I said.

We each held up our glasses and toasted to "we never do".

I had been drinking all day at the bar, that by the time it started filling up with people I didn't notice. I turned off my phone, knowing that she would soon be looking for me. About five more rounds and six shots in, I felt a hand on the back of my neck. The hand was soft, but it was squeezing the shit out of me. I turned around to see who the hand belonged to and it was her. Her face showed anger, frustration and disappointment.

"SO THAT'S IT HUH? YOU JUST GIVE UP AND RUN AWAY?"

Before I could respond, she interrupted me.

"YOU MEN ARE ALL THE DAMN SAME! ALL AFRAID TO LOVE AND BE LOVED! I JUST GIVE AND GIVE AND WHAT DO I GET IN RETURN? NOT A DAMN THING!"

"But I did leave you," I said. "I only came here to breathe and think."

BULLSHIT! You were on your way out and you just got caught is all.”

I could hear the pain in her voice. I felt bad. I really did, but I knew that this was the only way. A tear rolled down that beautiful golden face of hers.

“I never want to see you again! My friends were right. NEVER FUCK A WRITER!”

She stormed out and even though it was a painful moment, it was the most fitting one for us. Or so I thought. The bartender and the old timer both looked at me.

“This one’s on me,” said the bartender.

“I guess now we know that you’ve loss the woman,” said the old timer.

“Life doesn’t come with instructions,” I said.

Then we all toasted to that.

The Early Bird Gets The Worm

We were laying in bed naked. We had just gotten done fucking. She came twice, while I came once. Our bodies were in sync now more than ever. I was sitting up drinking straight from the bottle and that's when she asked me.

"Do you fuck all of your women like this?"

"What do you mean by that?"

"You know. Those you meet in the bars and those who tries to contact you, from admiring your work."

"I'm not sure how to answer that or if there's a specific response you're looking for, but I just do what I can, how I can and while I can."

"Hmm. I know we just met and I'm not sure why I'm even telling you this right now, but all I ask of you is that you always be honest with me. I cannot stand a liar and men seem to always show me that, just when I start to fall."

"I understand. It's easier for me to be honest from the start, than to lie. I have a terrible memory for one. Also, I just don't have the energy to put into the effort of lying."

She smiled and so did her eyes. I observed her and was in awe. Her nose was tiny, but fat. Her hips stuck out as if they were expanding. She had beautiful legs that had no scars or hair on them. Her small little bush between her thighs was well kept. It had a nice trim and shape up. I could feel myself rising up again.

"Hey, eyes up here Mr."

I shift my focus back on her eyes, as she instructed. I could feel her staring right into my heart. Our eyes locked, but I lips said nothing. I was staring so hard that I was beginning to see the small little scars underneath the makeup she used to hide them. I knew that she wanted me to kiss her, but instead I kept my distance.

"Did you just fart?" She asked.

"No, why?" I said.

"Something stinks."

"Oh hell I'm sorry. I left the window opened and sometimes the smell from the outside sewer would travel in here."

I got up and closed it.

"Hand me the bottle now. You've been hogging it all to yourself."

I handed it to her and got myself a cigarette. Lit it, took a long drag, then exhale. I watched her take swig from the bottle.

"Do you know what they say about writers in my city?"

"No, what?" I asked.

"That they are full of shit. ALL OF THEM! The intellects, the underground street poets, spoken word artists, the ones who drink, smoke or do any type of drug for inspiration. Complete assholes, who think they're hot shit. So I guess my reason for saying all of this is I'm curious to know which one are you?"

"First of all, let me just say this. I agree. If you're asking what category I fall under, then I don't have an answer for that. That is something for you to perceive on your own. Writing isn't some goddamn math problem. For me it's either like the river that flows or the fire that can't be tamed, so no one can touches it, until it burns out on its own."

The look on her face showed that she was taken aback by my response. She took another swig from the bottle, while I took another hit of my cigarette.

"Have you ever been in love before or fallen for one of your readers?"

"I've only been in love once, but it turned into obsession soon after. Although there were no physical abuse, there surely was a lot of emotional abuse. It led to things becoming ugly for the both of us. So I'm not sure if it was really love. Maybe it was just lust, mixed with my desire to have and be in love."

"I understand. Do you think the next time you get in a relationship it will be different?"

"Of course. Nobody who have experienced any form of a relationship remains the same. Whether we notice it or not."

She sat in silence and so did I. The room filled up with peace, with the exception of the sounds coming from our stomachs. She placed the bottle on the nightstand and put her head down and mouth on top of my pole. The inside of it was warm and wet. She was so good at it. Her teeth find scrape me at all and was very theatrical with the sounds she made. I kept looking down at her and watching her head go up and down. There was so much wetness that I could feel it sliding down underneath my ballsack. She was good with her hands as well. Giving me two handed twisted massages, while she glanced up at me with those demonic eyes. Her eyebrows were a bit long and she had a mole underneath her left eye. I placed my hand in her hair and put it up into a ponytail. I've always enjoyed seeing women with their hair up into a ponytail, over having it hang down. There's just something about it that drove me over the top. I was in control over her head, while it felt like she was in control of my spirit. She pulled it out of her mouth and slapped it against her face and lips.

"Bend over," I said.

She formed an arch with her body and it revealed her long torso. I ran my fingers across her fat cunt and felt the throbbing of her clitoris. She was ready for me to take her, but I wanted to tease her for a bit. It was something about making a woman quiver, before embracing her. The lead up is always more beautiful. The same with life. She let out soft moans and grip the bedsheets tightly. The more she moaned, the harder I got. He stood up strong and tall, waiting for me to give him the sign. I took him and ran the head over her sanctuary. I could see the veins forming in her arms and hands. The arch in her back grew deeper. I finally slid him inside her and it felt just as it did in her mouth. I pulled him out of her and took my tongue to write on the inside of her walls, as if I was writing scriptures of poetry. Her moans grew louder. Her breathing got heavier.

"OH MY GOD!"

I came back up and slid him back in with ease. I started with slow and long strokes. Then my strokes got deeper and a bit more fast pace. I looked down and saw the cream of her on me. The sounds coming from her insides were just as the sound of macaroni being stirred. It was absolutely beautiful to hear and see. I shifted my strokes and aimed for different areas inside of her.

"DAMN BABY," she screamed. "Give me all of you."

It was a pleasure to be in control. It was my true nature to be a dominant. I preferred my women to be submissive and let me lead. I begin hitting certain spots that had awaken the demon inside of her even more.

"I'M 'BOUT TO CUM! OHH I'M COMING!"

She screamed and shook. I kept stroking, while she came. Not long after her I came. I fell forward onto her and we laid like that. With me on top of her, until I got up to get a warm washcloth and washed us both off.

"Whew! That was so damn good! You're very smooth at what you do, but shitty when it comes to love."

"I'm still evolving in both areas," I said.

"I believe you, so don't worry. . .We all are actually."

"I like your hands," I said.

"I like your eyes and cheekbones," she said.

I got back in bed, grabbed her by the waist and laid in a spooning position, until we both fell asleep. It was 9AM and the sun had come through the halfway closed up blinds.

Cattleya

It was pure hell. Lorraine had just left my apartment storming out. She had broken dishes and ripped up my paintings before her departure. We were on bad terms and had been for months. Though, neither of us wanted to leave. We'd have some moments where the wine was thicker than the blood and those were the good times. However, we would run into the belly of the beast where the madness was stronger than the passion. It was downright ugly. The neighbors would call the cops and they would come knocking. I would answer the door in only my boxers and say in a gentle voice "oh no officer. Everything's fine". This time I think she's really gone. I wanted to write, but I knew that a poem couldn't save me. She left her heart, but took her wits and guts. I sat there in the chair, drinking cold beer and eating cold pizza, since she also took my microwave. Lorraine was such a gorgeous woman, with a soft soul. She had kind eyes, but could make a direct hit with that left hook of hers. She was on of those free spirited women, but still loyal to the soil. No matter where she went, she never forgot where she came from. Sometimes she would walk around the house in only a crop top and small shorts that cut off at the upper end of her thighs. She'd be singing and prancing all around. I would just sit there and admire those lovely legs of hers and that genuine spirit. As I said before, some days were pure hell and some days were heaven, but I appreciated and embrace them all, to be able to understand her. The thing about her was that she knew how to make love, carry love and share love. That was rare for me to find in a person and she had all three. I sat up drinking all night in my chair and thinking of her. The next morning came and I was still in my boxers and she was still gone. A bit of despair rushed onto my face. I went outside and stared at the grass, until I was struck with an idea. I went back inside and threw on some clothes and shoes. I figured that I would plant a flower in the name of Lorraine and by the time it reaches a good length, maybe she would be back. So everyday I nurtured it, watered it, gave it shade when needed and sometimes even talked to it. Weeks went by. Then the weeks turned into months and soon a year. Still no her. I cried. My heart couldn't take it. I grabbed the cutters and went outside to take the life of the flower. As I was about to clip it, a red car pulled up and out of it came a woman wearing dark shades and a big round hat. She walked up, then lifted her head.

It was Lorraine.

"I want you to know that I didn't come back for you, but just to invite you to my wedding."

She placed the invitation into my hand, then walked off.

That was the last time I saw her or that flower.

Redrum pt.1

Jack came into the bar. Fred was sitting at his usual spot, drinking a Jim Beam and coke.

"Where's my money Fred?"

"I don't have it yet man."

"Shit it sure does look like you do. You're up here buying shots for everyone and their goddamn mother."

"I just got lucky on a pick-up game is all."

"You better have my money tomorrow or else."

"FUCK YOU! No one threatens Fred G you bastard. You'll get your money whenever karma comes for me bitch!"

Jack said nothing and walked out of the bar with a smirk on his face. The bartender looked over at Fred and shook his head.

"The next time he comes in here, you guys better take that shit outside you hear? We don't need none of that up in here."

"Yeah yeah. Just fix me up another one and make it stronger this time."

Fred was hammered. So hammered that he couldn't even move from his seat to go piss. He down his shot and whipped out his pole underneath the table to let loose. It shot out fast, hard and warm. A woman who sat at the opposite side of the bar walked over towards him.

"Hey baby, how 'bout buying me a drink?"

"I only have enough money for my drinks."

"It'll be worth it in the end. If you know what I mean."

"All right. Tony, get the lady whatever she's drinking."

"Thanks doll. I'll be back. I need to go to the ladies room."

She walked away and Fred was staring at that huge ass of hers. It swayed with each step and he was memorize by it. The place grew quieter, with very few people in there. Though, Fred didn't take notice and was in a different place mentally. Jack walked back in, wearing long trench coat, a beanie and very tall boots. He walked up to Fred. . .

"Karma sent me."

(gunshot)

Teeth pt.1

(Dial tone)

"Hello?"

"Hey, it's me."

"Me who?"

"The me you had your dick inside of last night."

"Oh, what's going on?"

"I was wondering if you wanted to go out and grab some brunch. The day is beautiful and I figured we could have a nice meal and enjoy each others presence."

"Could we reschedule? I'm just not feeling too good right now."

"Oh okay. Well, I hope you get better soon."

"Thanks."

A week goes by and I haven't put any effort in to seeing her. The phone rang and it's from a number that I've never seen before. I thought that it might've been from this guy who I was doing business with. So I answered.

"Why the fuck haven't I heard from you?"

"I've been busy, sorry."

"So have I, but that doesn't mean that you can't make time for those I care about."

"I'll make it up to you. How 'bout we hangout this weekend? I will call you on Friday, to confirm. Is that okay?"

"I'm really trying to keep my hope and patience alive here, but okay."

Friday came and there was no phone call. She had gone out with her girls for drinks around 3pm.

"He still hasn't call, but maybe he will tonight. I'm going to give him until then."

Nighttime came and still no confirmation from him. She was sitting at home, when the phone rang. She raced to answer it.

"HELLO?"

"HEY BITCH! Do you want to go out? I just got invited to this party where the drinks are free for women!"

"I was waiting for an important phone call."

"Baby if they haven't called already, then they probably won't call until tomorrow."

"Well. . ."

"Bitch! FREE DRINKS!"

"All right all right."

The night goes on. It's now midnight and still nothing from him. She sat drinking and trying not to think about him, but the disappointment sat heavy on her mind.

"He really didn't call."

Saturday arrived and the flowers bloomed beautifully. She got dress and took herself out for brunch. The place she chose had dim lighting and was crowded. Every table was full. The music was very melancholy, with vintage wallpaper all around. She waited to be seated.

"How many?"

"Just one," she said.

"Follow me."

She got seated and ordered a mimosa. She looked over the menu twice, before noticing a woman sitting across from her with two small children. Their smile was pure and precious. It warmed her heart. The thought of her having her own someday entered her mind. A man with broad shoulders comes back to sit with them. His back is facing her. She instantly recognized the frame and get's up to make sure that the thought she had in her mind wasn't false. . .

"It's him."

1996 pt.1

The orange suns now going down and it was just her and myself inside the trailer. I could hear the sound of drums banging and being played by her brother and the loud laughter coming from my little sister. The room was small, with thin wooden walls. I could smell the old scent coming from the air vent. The sound of IMX blasting through the speakers, reminding me that it was summer in Alabama. I sat on her bed and got comfortable. She came in, then shut the door and locked it behind her. All 300lbs of her walked towards me, as I watched those wide heavy feet make contact with the wooden floor. The floor made a noise with each step. Her thick hand and fat fingers ran across my raw, thin and youthful face. She got up and went towards the radio. The sight of her made me uncomfortable. My eyes bled with worry. The longer I sat in her bed the deeper I started to sink in it. Here I was, sitting in what looked as if a whale had been killed in it. My small eyes observed her every movement, yet my young mind had no idea what was taking place. She came over to sit next to me. Once she sat, the bed shook without effort. She put her hand on the back of my neck. I could feel the dryness of them, which reminded me of fish scales. That large and heavy hand weighing down my scrawny neck. Her grip became tighter, as my lungs begin to scream for air. Using all 60lbs of me to try to make an escape, I thought that I would make it, but she overpowered me with her strength and weight. Suddenly, I felt a fist go across my face and fell back on top of the bed. She climbed up on top of me and sat herself up in a dominant position. I could feel all of her weight on my chest now. I gasped for air. The thought of death was about to become a reality. My heartbeat grew rapidly and louder. I could no longer hear the music. I tried to scream, but no one could hear me. I tried to fight once more, but she hit me with another blow across the face. I laid there in silence, as tears rolled down my face. Staring at the ceiling, hoping for something or someone to save me from this horrible reality. Then it began. This warmth and wetness that was on me. I lift up her stomach and saw death. Or at least that's what I thought, because I had no idea what it was or this feeling. Whatever it was, I knew that it wasn't right. Through my watery eyes I could see her dark face. The sharp knife cheekbones and that cruel smile piercing down at me. I could hear the tiny screws underneath the bed sounding as though they were going to come out and the bed would break. They were holding on for dear life, (just as I) while she continued fulfilling her desire. The grip of hers grew tighter. Her moans reminded me of a wild bear. Her breathing was now louder than the music. I knew now that no one was coming to save me. Not even God. She finished and got up to go wash off. My body felt like a used up fruit. Six years old and I've cried more than the average man already. I didn't bother to look down to see what she did. I put on my clothes and rushed out of the door, with tears in my eyes and the wind slapping against my face. When I got home, I tried to tell my godfather, but all he did was laugh and say, "You should be lucky. You just got your first piece of pussy". She took from me that day, more than she think. The only thing is, I'm still alive to write about it.

Leaving Things Behind

There were strings of her hair still there on my bedsheets. The condom wrapper that sat on the floor from the night before. Empty wine glasses and wine bottles, socks, underwear, work pants, books and some left open chips on the floor. We met at a party, then came back to my place for a couple of drinks. A quirky young woman, who had very long legs and stood 5'9. She was a depressed soul, who still had light inside of her and a successful career. Unlike myself, who was a depressed soul and was still hungry for having my writing looked at by a publisher. We were both full of chaos. Both of us looking to feel just a little peace at least. In the kitchen sink were dishes piling up. Last night we fucked once, then again around four am early morning. Two souls stripping themselves of thought and judgement. She left me stories about how she became who she is now and her family's background. I remember looking into those eyes of hers and seeing the passion and pain in them, as she was talking about her upbringing. Tears started forming in them and I could feel a taste of her trauma. She gave me the blues. She left her scent on my blanket. The sound of her voice lingered on throughout my apartment. My bedroom walls could still remember the shape of her face, when we were having sex. Her moans were still there in the cracks of my ceiling. The fingerprints she left all over my room now took over the emptiness. Underneath the bed was her red panties she also left behind.

"Damn, This woman sure knew how to leave shit behind. I wonder how many men she's left behind also," I thought.

I went and got a beer from the fridge, then sat at the typewriter to write about her.

Bear Hugs

I was sitting inside of the coffeeshop waiting on Carl. He had phoned me late last night about meeting him here to talk about something important. I arrived early, so I got a cup of coffee. About an hour went by and Carl still hadn't shown up.

"Where in the hell is he?"

This wasn't like him. Normally, he'd beat me here. I gave him a call again, but he didn't pick up. I ordered another cup of coffee and tried to piece together what he wanted to speak on. I had no idea what he was going to say. With Carl, one could never tell what he had going on. I looked over and saw a woman who looked to be on her mid 40s. She wore a dress that stopped about midway on her thigh. She was sipping her coffee slow and eating her muffin passionately. Her face was quite captivating. She had very seductive eyes and sat with her legs crossed, revealing a portion of her thigh.

"Would you like some more coffee?"

"Oh sure."

I had got so distracted that I didn't noticed the waitress's presence.

"Are you okay? You seem very distracted in something intense."

"I'm all right. Just waiting for someone."

"Dates are always running late."

"Oh no it's not a date. I'm waiting on a buddy of mine, who told me to meet him here."

"What is his name or what does he look like? Maybe I can help you out with that."

"His name is Carl and has a very welcoming face, with dark brown eyes, a low cut and a beard so thick that if you stuck your hand inside it would get lost."

"Oh you're talking about C-Lo."

"C-Lo?"

"Yeah. He comes in here quite often actually."

"When was the last time you saw him?"

"Hmm. . .Yesterday, I think. Yeah, it was yesterday. He seemed very odd. Almost anxious and worried. Is something wrong?"
"That's what I'm trying to find out myself. Carl has never done this before. Sure he may be a madman sometimes, but this takes the cake here."

"Well, if you need anything else, let me know."

"Thank you."

"Anytime sweets and this one is on the house."

I left a tip on the table and left. She was such a good look, but I had no time to indulge in her. I had to figure out where Carl was and what he had to tell me. I went down to a couple of places I thought he might be. His barber, the woman who he always showed affection for, his favorite bar and even some of his old gang that he used to hang around. All said the same thing.

"I haven't seen him."

I went to the park to watch the ducks and clear my head. I thought about Carl and how he still haven't phoned me back. I hated being left on the edge. I tried to think about the possibilities of why Carl needed to talk. My mind was blank. I felt like a wanderer who had reached a dead end. I reflected on the memories of Carl and how he accepted me for who I am. Crooked teeth and all. The sun hadn't set yet. It was still pretty early, so I still had time to find him. I got in my car and drove home. When I got home I cracked open a beer and hit the typer. I had to bleed the soul and release the thoughts in my mind. Also, I was working on a new book. I was writing a story about a boy who was going though a traumatizing experience from being raped by his babysitter. He was a black boy, who's life was full of pain and trials. I was getting down to the meat of the story, when there was a knock at my door. I went to go check and see who it was. Looking through the small peephole first. It was Carl's fling.

"Hey, sorry to bother you, but have you seen Carl? I've been looking for him since earlier this morning."
"I haven't, but I'm looking for him as well."

"Oh geez. Do you mind if I use your bathroom?"

"Go right ahead. It's right there on the right."

She entered and walked to the bathroom. While she was in the bathroom, I grabbed myself an empty glass and a bottle of wine. As I was pouring the wine, she came out.

"I hope you have two glasses," she said as she laughed.

"This one's yours."

I got up to grab another glass and poured one for myself.

"So did he give you any clue as to where he was going?"

"No. The last thing we spoke about was how he wanted to escape his reality. As I said before, he was acting really strange. He kept going on about how sad he was, which I thought was even more concerning. Considering the fact that Carl RARELY gets sad. So we were hanging out yesterday, over at his favorite coffeeshop, then went back to my place. We got really cross-faded. We smoked, drank, made love, then fell asleep. When I woke up he was gone. I figured that maybe he had gone out to get some more to drink and smoke, but time went on and he still wasn't back yet. I stayed up all night, just to see if he would come back. Morning came and I grew tired of waiting. So I went back over to the coffeeshop and asked if he had been there, but the woman who usually seats us said that she hadn't seen him. That now has led me to being here with you. I figured you might've seen him, knew where he might've been or heard from him."

She sat with her legs crossed, taking sips of her wine. She had a nice set of hands that held the wine glass with class. I could tell that she was a woman with standards and elegance, but had a touch of madness to her.

"Unfortunately, I haven't. Hopefully, he turns up soon. I'm worried about him."

"Well, if he shows up, could you have him give me a call?"
"Sure thing."

She finished up her drink, then left.

That night I thought about Carl. I couldn't sleep a lick. Tossing and turning all night, trying to keep my eyes shut. I started counting the sheep, but sleep was nowhere to be found. About an hour went by and I was beginning to fall asleep, when there was a knock at the door. I looked over at the clock and hit read 12:45AM. I got up and went to the door. I guess whoever was on the other side of it grew impatient, because the knocks got louder.

"I'M COMIN' DAMN!"
I opened up the door and in comes flying Carl. He looked like he had been through rain, sleet and hell.

"Normal people say hello whenever they enter someone else's home," I said.

"Well, then I guess I'm not normal. Where's your phone? I need to make a call."

"It's over there, but why are you in such a rush?"

He ignored my response.

"Umm, yes. I would like to confirm my flight and see what time does it fly out? Uh huh. Okay thanks!"

He hung up, then turned around and looked directly at me. I could sense the paranoia and see it in his eyes. I saw the sweat dripping from his forehead onto my carpet.

The collar of his shirt looked as if it was screaming for help, with how worn out and dirty it was looking. His shoes had no shoelaces and his jeans were full of holes. There was something Carl was not telling me and I needed to find out.

"Two things I need to know Carl."

"What's up?"

"What did you have to talk about and where have you been?"

He looked at me disgusted and as if I had offended him.

"You got a cig?"

"Yeah, I do, but you're only getting it if you tell me what the hell is going on."

"All right all right."

I went and got the cigarette for him and got myself one too. I poured two whiskey's with two ice cubes in each, then we lit our cigarettes.

"My reason for not showing up to the coffeeshop involves what I had to tell you. So, well as of lately, I've been seeing these people outside of my window at night. Every night around 7PM, it's the same people. People who I've never met before. Just outside staring at my window, with dark circles around their eyes. It's kept me up all night and I don't know what else to do. I know that it sounds crazy, but it's the truth I tell ya'! I need to escape, but in a lowkey fashion. I have a place in mind, but I can't tell you where until I reach my destination. I know you won't tell anyone, but right now, I can't trust a soul. I'll be sure to write you, so be looking out for my letters. I can't explain everything right now, since I don't have much time. So far now, let's just enjoy our drinks and cigs. In time, all things will reveal the truth."

I wanted more from him, but I understood that he had his reasons. I knew there was no way of convincing him and I wasn't going to try to. So I trusted him.

"By the way, your fling dropped in looking for you."

"Did she have childbearing hips and strong facial features?"

"Uh huh."

"Oh that's Whitney. She's such a nice girl. Do you want her?"

"What the hell man?"

"Just asking haha."

"Hell I have enough women problems in my life. I don't need anymore. If I shit wrong or piss sideways I'm fucked. No thanks."

"I hear you on that one. Well, if you could, look out for her please. We met at a grocery store a few months ago and she's been loyal to the soil ever since."

"I gotcha."

We drank and smoked a few more cigarettes, before he left. Weeks went by and still no letter. I released a new book of short stories. It did okay, still not enough to take me out of the gutters. Though I still celebrated with a pack of beers, a box of fried chicken with fries and a bottle of wine. As I was drinking, eating and listening to some Jazz, there was a loud bang on my door.

"People just love to knock hard."

I was expecting for it to be Carl, but it was his fling.

"Sorry. It's me again, but has he. . ."

Her eyes grew bigger and her mouth dropped open. I wasn't sure why, but then I felt the wind from outside on my balls. I realized that I didn't have any bottoms on.

"Excuse me, while I go put on some pants. You can come in and shut the door behind you."

I came back out with pants on.

"So has he come by or even called?"

"Nope. Not a beep."

"I went by his place to see if he'd be there, but he wasn't. I'm beginning to worry more and more now."

I looked over at my clock and it read 2:43AM.

"Don't worry. I know Carl and that guy is fighter. He has such a tough spirit that drives him. Also, a sense of humor to match. Would you like a drink?"

"Sigh. . .Sure."

I made the drinks and we shared a moment.

"So would you mind telling me why you were naked or is that just how you prefer to lounge around?"

"I had a feeling you would bring that up sooner or later in our connection."

"I mean, I had to. It wasn't a bad sight. I'm just curious."

She gave a light, but sentimental smirk. I had an idea of what she must've been thinking.

"I'm working on my new book."

"So you must be naked whenever you write?"

"In a sense, yes. It's a bit of peace and freedom."

"I see. So why did you go and put on pants, if that is going to hinder your true nature?"

"To make us both comfortable."

"I'm comfortable and I was before then."

We sat there in silence and drank. Staring at one another, then at the wall. She has good taste, but I believe that her mind is clouded right now, because she doesn't know where Carl is.

"If free is what you desire, then free it shall be."

She got undress on down to her panties and bra. I looked at her well shaped figure and quickly took notice to the amazing job that God had done with her. It was all there. Everything laid perfectly.

"Can we go to bed together? I don't want to be alone tonight. Plus, I'm drunk," she said.

I looked at her in silence, without responding.

"Please. I just really need to be held tonight."

"All right."

We got in bed and got in the spooning position. I thought that it was going to be a long night of me tossing and turning, but surprisingly it wasn't. As soon as our heads hit the pillows, we were both out cold.

I awoke to a long loud knock on my door.

"DAMMIT! Doesn't anyone ever let a man sleep around here?"

When I got to the door it was the mailman. He gave me this envelope, then walked off. I went into the bathroom and sat on the toilet to read what was inside.

Dear Sin,

How are you holding up you bastard? I hope all is well and the words are flowing like red wine. As for me, well I'm her in this shithole ward. To tell you the truth, I shouldn't call it that, since I have been making progress in here. When I was on the outside, (I said that as if I'm in jail haha) I had no sense of direction. Being cooped up in the psych (that's what we call it) has taught me a lot. I won't go into details right now, but I will in my next letter. I left Whit some money, which she'll probably receive in about a day or two. Make sure she get herself something nice to wear and lots of food. It should be enough, because I stored some dough away just for her in this situation. Sin, my dear brethren, look after her for me please. Besides you, she is the only good thing to happen to me in this world. I don't want her to go out into the streets searching for warmth, love, food or anything else. You and I BOTH come from the streets. So we know exactly how those streets are. I have to do this thing out on my own, but until I get there, be there for her. I am aware of her need and cravings for intimacy and affection. I give you my blessing to fulfill her needs and desires.

I love you my brethren. Never forget that.

with love,

Carl

I handled the rest of my business up in the bathroom, then went and laid back down next to Whit. Her body was warm as ever and skin was softer than a baby's eyes.

Loose Strings

I was sitting there at the typewriter working on this piece, with a bottle of Jack next to me, thinking about my next move in life. She was in the bedroom watching the news.

"Babe? Can you come in here for a second?"

"Yeah, give me a sec," I said.

I finished up a section and got up to go check to see what she wanted.

"Yeah?"

"Did you see what happened?"

"No, I didn't."

"Come here."

I got closer to her.

"These damn tools have broken into the Capitol Building. They are PISSED to see their beloved orange chicken leave the Oval Office."

She was showing me on her phone and sure enough, the racists fools had finally revealed their true form. There were some even climbing walls to get inside. Others broke and smashed windows. It was totally madness. The entire world was all watching. So many headlines from all over. It was disappointing, but not surprising, since I always knew that this was what this country was molding for years.

"Now, had this been black people, they would've been let it rip. No questions asked. This fucking country makes my ass itch."

I walked in the kitchen and got two empty glasses, dropped three ice cubes in each of them. I grabbed the bottle of jack and went back into the bedroom. I poured us both a drink.

"Thank you baby, because after seeing all of this shit I'm definitely going to need this."

What do we toast to?" She asked.

"To chaos," I said.

We clanked our glasses and took a nice sip.

"Does anything ever rattles you?" She asked.

"Of course! The thing is, I'm just not that move by things that I am aware of."

"Do you see yourself living here in America for the rest of your life?"

"I'm not sure. If I had a choice I'd probably be in Paris."

"Paris huh? I've been there before. It's not that it's cracked up to be, but it gets the artistic juices flowing. You know, even in chaos the world still shines its light onto beauty. That can't be said about a lot of things these days. Especially, love."

She took a long pause, as if she and her mind was elsewhere having their own conversation, then started back up.

"You know, love is full of shit. It starts off embracing and warm, then it leaves you cold and without. The beginning is always the same, but the ending never changes."

She took the bottle and poured us another round.

"By the way, how did we get on this subject about love?" She asked.

"I'm not sure," I said.

"It sure as hell is a peaceful night."

"Yes. Yes it is."

"Would you be upset if I fucked another guy?"

"Would you?" I asked.

"Would I what?" She asked.

"Would you fuck another guy?"

"I mean, I wouldn't. I just wanted to know how much you cared."
"You just love to get a FUCKING rise out of me don't you?"

"Why are you yelling?" She asked. "It was just a questioned."

"FUCK THAT! This is EXACTLY what you wanted, so now I'm going to give it to you. If you awake the sleeping demon, then you must deal with the havoc it will bring."

The argument went all downhill from there. Things were thrown, words were said and feelings were obviously hurt. She grabbed her things and stormed out without uttering another word.

It had been six weeks since we last spoken or been in the presence of one another. That last fight really put a dent in us. That day there was anarchy. That weekend I ran into an old buddy of mine, who told me that she had gotten lucky and shacked up with some rich muthafucka. Though I wasn't upset at her for it. Even if, she loves him or not. Sometimes, well often, it is us who destroys and poison our own fruits of labor.

Social Butterflies

They were all waiting. The publisher, the readers and supporters, the whores and the hood niggas. The women who admired me from afar, those who hung out with me from time to time and even those who hated my guts. They were all waiting on another book from me. They were all waiting to see what else I had to say and if there was anything left in the tank. Though I still didn't give them anything. You see, I had it. I just could not cough it up. It was so far down inside of me that I wasn't sure if I would be able to resurface it. So I got drunk each night, played Jazz records, fucked whenever I could from time to time and didn't touch the typewriter. All I did was stare at it and poured my emotions to it, as if it was my shrink. I wanted the typewriter to be my slut. I wanted it to be the most precious thing that I've ever paid for. Even more precious than pussy. The way the keys felt underneath my fingers, you would've sworn that the typewriter and myself was in a serious relationship. To tell you the truth, that was kind of how it was. I was the dom and it being the submissive one. We meshed well together. It got used to my sadness and drunk stories, while I became very fine of its screams. That was a while ago. Before this phase of my life. I haven't written in over a month. Hell I've probably masturbated more times than I've written, as of lately. It's not that I have writer's block or anything. It's just that the fuel is not there and I'm not one to force things. Especially, art and creativity. It has to flow. The only time I force shit is whenever I am on the toilet. Then sometimes you just have to. Force nothing, but feel everything.

One weekend night, I was at an old buddy's place. It was him Slick-T, his girlfriend Toya, her sister Lisa and her boyfriend Kel. We were all drinking and playing game called "Drunk UNO". Although I wasn't drunk yet, I could feel the warmth building up inside of me. Things were pretty calm, until Kel was beginning to feel himself a bit too much and became drunker than all of us. Now I'm all for a man drinking until he meet the gods, but damn. I don't want to have to babysit the fucker.

"You see the right here," he slurred out of his mouth.

"THIS RIGHT HERE NIGGA, IS MINE! If you look closely, you will see the name K.D. stamped on it."

He pointed in the direction of her crotch area. Lisa seemed embarrassed and put her head down.

"It stands for Kevin Drickson. Better known as KING DANGALING."

"UGH! Here we go with shit again. I hate it when he gets like this," said Lisa.

"You hate what?" Asked Kel.

"Nothing Kel baby."

"That's right. Now come over here and give me some sugar baby."

His words were so drunk that when he said, "sugar" it came out as "SUGA" instead.

"All right. Now let's get back to playing," said my buddy.

The game went on a few more rounds and by that time, Kel was bored of playing and went out with his friends. Is it was only Slick-T, Toya, Lisa and myself. The crazy thing about it, was how Lisa didn't seem to care at all by Kel leaving. Her face actually showed a sigh of relief. Now it was just the four of us.

"Now that the asshole is gone, let's make it interesting by steaming things up a bit," said Lisa. "Lets continue with Drunk UNO, but add stripping into the mix."

"I see somebody's feeling a little frisky tonight," said Slick-T.

"You damn right I am! I haven't been fucked in three months. Let alone arouse and touched. So I need some kind of intimacy." She looked over at me with those piercing eyes.

"You down?" She asked.

I contemplated at first, but then agreed shortly after.

The game began. After a couple of rounds we were each in our undergarments.

"Okay, next round winner takes all," said Toya.

It became my turn and I only had one card left. It was a Draw +4 and all I had to do was play it and the game would be over. Lisa and Toya both looked at me. Slick was staring at me as well. All waiting to see what I had. There was a part of me that didn't want to end them so quickly, but then there was also the part of me who didn't give a shit and wanted to see what lied behind those undergarments.

"AH COME ON," they shouted.

I laid down my card softly and watched their faces drop to their knees. Though for some reason, I think that this was what they wanted. To have a reason to free themselves and tease.

"Since we were the losers, we've decided to put on a little show for you guys. Sit in these chairs and get comfy."

We did as we were told.

The show they put on for us was far better than I expected. At one point, I thought that I was in a nightclub and it was only Lisa and myself. Toya and Slick and already gone upstairs to their bedroom. So that left Lisa and I alone by ourselves.

"Are you sure 'bout this?" I asked.

"Of course I am. Why wouldn't I be?"

"I don't know hell. Maybe, the fact that you have a boyfriend and you're here grinding on top of me."

"Hell he doesn't mind and as you can see, his ass is not even here to give me what I desire. So it's nobody's fault, but his own."

She planted her lips onto mine and we were in sync. Our tongues swiping away like two swords. I could feel the wetness of the inside of her mouth. Feeling the sharpness of her strong teeth. It was starting to steam up a bit. It had gotten so intense that the chair that we were sitting in had broken, yet we continued on. As we were getting to it, a soft voice from a few feet away approached us with, "May I join?"

It was Toya.

She was drunk, naked and ready. She stood there with all that body effortlessly showing. Not only that, but it was glowing with oil. She had smooth skin and a lot of curves.

"What happened to Slick?" asked Lisa.

"Girl his old tired ass passed out on me, while I was oiling myself up. I couldn't revive him whatsoever."

Lisa looked at me.

"I'm not sure if Slick would be cool with that," I said.

"Oh he wouldn't mind at all. If he was up he'd probably join in as well."

Lisa looked at me again.

"Sigh. . .All right."

She smiled, then strutted over slowly. Instantly, we all clicked. Imagine, a Royal Rumble between a lion, a tiger and a bear. All roaring and discovering new heights of ourselves, without judgment.

The next morning, I had two beautiful women on the side of me. Neither of them were mine. I got up to sneak out early and left them both there to sleep. I didn't know what was to come next, but I was ready to accept whatever. When I got home I took a hot shower, put on a pot of coffee, poured myself a cup and went straight to the typewriter to type. I took my first sip and thought about last night interactions and exchanges. I sat and reflected on both of them. Not just the sex part, but how unhappy they both seemed before the sex. Both of them were quite comfortable and so quick to open up to me. It sure as hell was a sight to see and an experience to embrace. I poured myself another cup and drank. I sat there and hit the keys. I typed up four short stories and a couple of poems to go along with those stories. I was going to mail them off tomorrow. I figured my time had come to an end with Slick and company, so I didn't bother showing my face around there anymore.

A few weeks later, Slick phoned me.

"What's up man?"

"Same ol' same," I said.

"I know that shit's real. Listen. . ."

"I wonder what is he about to say."

"Everyone was wondering what happened to you. Specifically, Lisa. We couldn't find you this morning. So everyone was worried. I calmed everyone down and told them that you are a recluse, so you will most likely always do that. Anyway, I wanted to invite you out for drinks. Are you down?"

"Thank you, but I'm hitting the keys at the moment. Plus, I'm low on dough."

"No worries at all. That's what I'm here for. I got you. It's my treat.

"Well, in that case. . ."

"Meet me downtown at this bar called, "SHAKEYS".

"All right I'll give you a ring, once I wrap up this story."

Short Flames With No Names

I think people are more fond of the idea of me, rather than actually me. They go after the pieces of me that they want, then leave. I have been single for seven years now and haven't fucked in almost five months. She was broken and drunk like me that night. We met at this gathering for artists, writers and musicians. I didn't really mingle much. In fact, I didn't want to be there, but Someone I knew invited me. I got drunk, ate some of their very expensive food and people watched. The women all looked bored to be there and the men all seemed to be stroking each other's egos. It looked like a scene from a bad low budget horror film, with terrible actors. We were all there for a reason. Either to get drunk, for free food, to network and get signed or to get laid. All and all, we were each there for something. She came up to me wearing this tight fitted dress that showed her figure gracefully. Her legs were well moisturized and her hair was up in a ponytail, which made her facial features standout more. She was blessed with lovely hands. A walking piece of art she was, that came alive that night.

"Hey don't I know you?" She asked.

"I don't believe so," I said.

"Are you sure? Are you not the author of the book 'All The Leaves Turned Orange'?" She asked.

"Maybe."

"Why are you over here alone?"

"I'm not alone. You all are still here."

"I see we have ourselves a comedian. I'm Bev."

"Pleasure to meet you. I'm Sinclair. So which one of these dull heads are you here with?"

"Oh I work for myself honey. I guess you can say I'm with myself, representing myself. I own one of the largest publishing companies in town. You may or may not have heard of us." "The Little Red Sweater Publishing Company"

In fact, I did hear of them. They were a company that was on the come up. They had published a few of the top authors, who were now getting their work shown everywhere. I wasn't there yet, but was hoping to get there. She continued talking.

"But it doesn't really matter if you have or not. What matters now is the fact that you're over here all alone. Why is that?"

"I just prefer to be alone that's all. I was invited to come, so that I could meet and greet to get more exposure. From the look of this, if I have to be like any of these uptight ass people in here just to be published, then to hell with that shit."

She laughed hard and slap herself on the knee. I stared down at those hands of hers to get to get a closer look at them. They were even more gorgeous up close. The veins in them were forming themselves as art that had interlocked. I could also smell the fragrance she had on. It was a warm sensation. It amazed me how she spoke so gentle, but laughed so aggressive.

"Well, I can definitely tell that you are not like them. So what would you categorize your style of writing?"

"I would say transgressive literature and confessional poetry."

"Those both sound like very intriguing topics. Though I'm honestly not too familiar with them. Care to share a more detail version of them?"

"Let's just say that my work is filthy, raw, vulnerable, with a drop of kindness in it."

"Hmm. . .Sounds like something I would definitely enjoy getting my hands on. Where can I read some of your work? Do you have a business card or a book with you now?"

"Unfortunately, I do not. Although, you can find them at a Barnes & Nobles, online at Amazon or back at my place I have a few."

"Okay. Do the online copies come with your signature?"

"They do not, but I can sign them for you, once you get receive them."

"I think I'd much rather buy them directly from you. To support a black man who writes. Can you drop by my office on Friday, around noon?"

"Sure. Where is your office located?"

"On Franklin street downtown. Right across from that huge church."

"Oh okay. I think I may know where that is."
"Here. Take my number. If you get lost, give me a ring and I'll guide you."

She walked away and I saw that tight fitted dress hug her ass with passion. I wanted to unlock her full potential that night.

As the night went on, the crowd of uptight talking assholes became more and more uninteresting. One woman was so drunk that the guy who she came with had left her by her lonesome. She didn't seem to notice or care. I was coming back from the open bar, when she stopped me.

"And who the hell are you? I haven't seen you here before. Wait a goddamn minute! Is that Sweet Dick Willy? My my my, how you've grown into such a beautiful young man. Quick! Give me a taste of you, before my husband comes back. If he catches us, then all hell will break loose and he'll kill us both for sure. Especially, you."

"Look sweets, I'm not who you think I am and your husband won't lay a finger on me. Now if you will, excuse me."

I walked off and got lost within the crowd. Some people were dancing. Some were sitting back laughing, talking or complaining about the food or the music. Over in the corner was a woman standing by herself. I went to the bar for two drinks, then over to her.

"Here. Maybe this'll help," I said.

"How did you. . .?"

"Don't worry. I saw you over here looking like me and figured that this place isn't big enough for two sad souls. So I decided to bring light to you and keep the darkness all to myself."

"But what if I like darkness?"

"That could be true, but can you handle it is the question."

"I've handled it this long. I can handle anything that swings my way."

I wish that I could say I was surprised by her response, but I wasn't. It's very rare for a woman to stand alone and those that usually do are very strong headed and independent individuals. There were sadness in the corner of her eyes. I'm not sure why, but I was always attracted to women who were either broken, sad, full of passion, with a bit of rage inside of them. They were the ones you knew that you could trust.

"Well, then, I guess there's no need for my presence," I said.

"At this very moment, no there isn't," she said.

I walked away. She was a cold bastard, with childbearing hips. To the naked eye, one might've thought that she was lonely in that corner, but coming from a place of understating I knew she that wasn't. I sat there, toasted to the rest of the night and continued drinking.

I had all of my books with me, waiting outside of her office. Her name Bev LeeAnn was on the office door in bold letters. Her secretary was a young woman, who looked as if she was still in college. Her breast sat up high underneath her button up shirt. She had on glasses and long straight hair. She moved her fingers fast across the keyboard of her computer and answered the phone directly after the second ring. I sat there waiting and watching the young secretary go to work. I could see it in her actions how passionate she was with her job. It was something to see, considering how many people in this world hated theirs.

"Mr. Sinclair, Ms. LeeAnn will see you now."

I got up and followed her through the double doors down the hallway into another set of double doors, until we reached one door that stood alone.

"Here he is Ms. LeeAnn. Would there be anything else for you?"

"Thanks! Hold my calls for today and cancel the rest of my appointments please."

"Yes ma'am."

The young secretary left us. For a couple of minutes there was silence. The room temp was very pleasant. I looked around observing the place. I quickly noticed how she didn't have any pictures on the walls or her desk. Normally, when you go into these types of places you see those things first.

"Sorry, I had to finish up this conference call first. Hello again and welcome. Would you like anything to drink? I have water, tea, beer, wine, whiskey, cognac and vodka."

"I'll take a glass of whiskey, neat please."

She poured two glasses of Jameson.

"All right. Here you go. Now where are the books?"

I handed them all to her. I continued drinking my drink and walking around the room looking at the furniture and built of it. While she was reading and I was taking a look around, the room fell silent again. We both focusing on the task at hand. For her, my books and for myself her office room. The office as kind of huge and spacious. I saw an area over in the corner that stood out to me. It was much darker than the rest of the room. I walked over to look at all the books she had on her shelf. She had a pretty good collection. There was some Bukowski, Baldwin, Angelou, Plath, Hemingway, Sexton and a few others. Next to it she had a record collection. I skimmed through. Fifteen minutes had gone by, then she finally spoke.

"WOW! This is really beautiful and so full of emotions, This is how a reader is supposed to be after they read a book. They are supposed to leave feeling SOMETHING! I'm going to buy every last one of them. How many are there?"

"Six so far, but I'm currently writing another one as we speak."

"I need that in my life! Your writing really does the soul good. Yeah, I need more time with you and your books."

The day rolled on into the night and suddenly, it was only the two of us left in the building. Even the cleaning crew had gone home now.

"You want to know something?"

I looked right into those sharp eyes of hers and nodded my head yes.

"It's been awhile since I've let a man make me smile. I'm usually a bitch, who works hard and only focus on herself."

"I guess you should let me make you smile more often," I said.

She put down her drink, then walked slowly over to me. I was sitting there still drinking from my glass. She bent down to take my drink from me and kissed my lips with aggression and warmth. We embraced without questions being asked. She pulled away for a second.

"I want you to fuck me, just as you did in one of the stories in your books. Give me the whole thing and don't hold back. Open up the hidden caves inside of me and make my office remember the scent of you and the sound of my moans. Let me swallow and feel all of you. Including, the demons you have."

I looked at her face and saw the serious in her. I lift her up and took her over to her desk and fucked her madly. While I was stroking, I looked around and saw over there, on top of the bookshelf high up, a picture of her. It looked like she had taken that when she was younger and fresh onboard. Tuh. I guess you really did have at least one picture in here.

We finished up, then headed out. I didn't have a car, so she drove me back to my place.

"Well, Mr. Sinclair, it's been a fun ride. I must say, you are your words. You're exactly like the love you write about in your books. Maybe we could do this again sometime."

"Yeah, maybe so. By the way, is Bev LeeAnn your real name?"

"Oh honey, names aren't important. Stories are."

I got out and watched her drive off into the late night.

Here We Go Again

When she walked in everyone in the bar took notice. Her face was thin, with cheekbones as sharp as knives. She stood tall at 5'11 and took long strides. She wore a tight blue dress, that had a split on the side. She had on these very tall high heels that showed off her long legs and calf muscles. Along with her was another woman, who was the heavier side. Her face was full and lovely to look art. Her thighs were thick like two soft pillows. She had on a very short skirt, which showed much of her lower half, a crop top button up and some black boots that had a fat sole. I was sitting at a table a few feet away from the bar. I watched them, as they walked up to the bar. All the men seem to hassle them and fight for their attention. Each of the women didn't seem too impressed with their efforts of the men. They ordered their drinks and sat there, with all of the eyes glued to them. I needed more to drink, so I went up to the bar and got a drink, a shot and a beer, then went back to my table. A new group of guys came up to the two women trying to win their hearts. All looked like working class men, who got their hands dirty and drank to stay alive and find something worth living for. Just as the men before them, they too were shun away as well. A few moments after that, another round of men came up to the women. This time, these men wore business suits and spoke very well. Although they looked very intelligent, they were dry and dull as an unused nail. Watching all of this, what I gathered from the two women was that they didn't give a shit about how much money you had, your fashion choices or how smart you tried to put off. It caught me by surprised, because those were usually the kind of things that most people went for. Those things and society's standards of beauty. The night went on and I continued going up to the bar, getting drinks and back to my table. This time around, I got my drink, sat it on my table, then walked over to use the restroom. In there was two guys who were drunk and plotting on how to get the two women at the bar.

"Say man, did you see those two shorties at the bar?"

"HELL YEAH I DID!"

"We gotta get at them. I want the tall one. You can get the short chubby thicker one."

"Why the hell do I gotta get that one? Why won't YOU get her and I'll get the taller one? I'm tired of covering for you. I sure as hell am tired of always ending up with the less appealing friend, while you go off with the beautiful one."

"All right all right. You can have the short one and I'll get the tall one. Happy now?"

"Sounds good for a change. Hold up! You're trying to pull a fast one on me. I said I will get the taller one and YOU get the shorter one.

"Okay. I'll take one for the team this time. Besides, I love short thick women. Especially, those who have a fupa."

They zipped, flushed and walked out without washing their hands. I zipped, didn't flush and washed my hands. There no paper towels to dry my hands, so I wiped them on my shirt. When I got back to my table, there was a fight going on at the bar, where the two women were sitting. I had a feeling that it was because of them. When the security broke it up, it was the two men who were in the restroom with me and the men who were in the business suits. The security tried to kick them all out, but one of them got free and hit one of the business men. All of a sudden, there was a large crowd around them and someone had thrown a drink, which struck up another fight. Beer bottles were thrown everywhere, along with fists. I sat there watching from my table, drinking and without a care in the world. Finally, the security had gotten it all under control and threw those involved out. I was low on beer, so I went up to the bar and was stopped by the two women this time.

"Excuse me," said the taller one.

"Yes," I responded.

"I just would like to say that you are the ONLY man in here who didn't try to hit on us tonight. First, I would like to say thank you. We greatly appreciate it, but we are curious as to why haven't you?"

"There are many reasons. I never go to a bar with the notion to pick up women. Another reason, it looked like you all were having a good time enjoying yourselves and I never want to disrupt someone else's fun, when I wasn't invited. Also, I'm not much of a people's person. I'd rather just do my own thing."

"Hmm. . .Will you please stay and have a drink with us? Maybe if you sit here with us, then those other guys would stop hitting on us."

"I would, but I have my own table over there and right now, it's too crowded up here at the bar."

"Yeah, you're right. Well, how's about we come over there with you?"

"All right."

An irritating noise of what sounded to be the ring of a bell.

"This is the last call for alcohol ladies and gentlemen. So if you would like to get your last round of drinks, I advise you to do it now."

"Aww man. We finally make a friend and now they're about to closed," said the tall one.

"We can leave here, pick up a case of beer and a bottle, then head back to my place," said the shorter one.

"Are you fine with that?" Asked the tall one.

"Sure thing," I said.

We drank our last round and got up to leave. When we made it to the front entrance of the bar, there was this group of men standing next to it. Almost blocking the exit.

"So you would rather leave with this lame, but not us?"

The guy who said it must've been someone who came up to them when I was in the restroom, because I didn't see him talk with them all night.

"Umm, excuse us please."

"YOU BITCHES AIN'T SHIT!"

I felt my fist tighten and out came a punch from me. I connected right with his jaw. I couldn't stop myself. I had forgotten all about his group of friends, who were punching me, but I didn't feel any of the throws. We were all tussling and ended up outside on the curb. I saw blood and thought that it was mine, but I didn't care and just kept fighting. Someone from inside of the bar came and broke it up. The two women ran up to me and we walked away, without looking back.

"Thank you for sticking up for us. We owe you big time. I gotta say, you're one crazy young man though."

"Oh it's all right, but he had it coming."

"You were getting DOWN!"

"Haha. What I can't figure out is how his friends got off of me."

"Oh didn't you see? We fought off his friends."

"REALLY?"

"HELL YEAH! It was the least we could do, after what you did for us."

"I had no idea. I honestly thought that you left me, which I wouldn't have cared."

They both just looked at me and continued walking. We got to the store and picked up what we came for. My wrist started bothering me.

"OH MY God, YOUR SHIRT," shouted the taller one.

We all looked down at it.

"I see blood, but no wounds," I said.

We looked all over to see if he had gotten me, but it must've been his blood, because I was wound free. The store clerk looked at us with disgust, but neither girls nor I really cared. They paid the man and we left. When we made it to our destination, which by the way, was a very long ass walk. We had to walk up some stairs to get to her place. When she opened it up, it smelled of cinnamon. A small dog ran up to us barking and sniffing each of us. I started to kick it, but I figured I'd let it live this time around.

"Where's your bathroom?" I asked.

"It's to the right, the second switch to turn on the light."

I went and hit the second switch. The light came on and I saw her bathroom. There was hair product all around and different types of moisturizers. I whipped it out and let loose. I had been holding in my piss, since before the fight. I zipped up, washed my hands and dried my hands on the towel she had hanging up.

I walked into the living room and they were already sitting down talking. There was a brown couch and a smaller version of it.

"I just realize that I don't know your names."

They both laughed very loudly and without shame.

"DAMN! That's funny, because we don't know yours either. I can't believe we just invited a total stranger to come back home with us haha."

"You're not a killer are you? I mean, I do like to be choked and all, but I would prefer to live through it," said the shorter one.

"Unfortunately, I don't have the guts to kill you," I said.

"Well, good then. So what is your name?"

"It's Sinclair and yours?"

"I'm Naomi and she's Xen with an X."

Naomi was the shorter one, while Xen was the taller one.

"Pleasure to meet you both and thanks for inviting me to drink with you."

"Shall we cheers?"

"To one HELL OF A NIGHT!"

We clanked glasses and downed the first round. Naomi poured another round and it was all laughter and drunken told stories from that point on. The conversations were a variety of things. There were talks about love, horoscopes, aliens, religion, God, satan, death, life, abuse of all kinds, romance and work life balance. We spoke on how each of us liked to be pleased. Well they did most of the talking, while I just sat there back and listened and drank. There were some tears, laughter, silence and comfort. It was pretty intense overall, but I preferred it that way.

"It's getting pretty late and I'm beat. It's been a long day, so I'm going to bed. You two don't mind do you?"

"Not at all," said Naomi.

"Nope."

"I'll see y'all in the morning."

I watched the petite frame of hers strut away. Those long legs had a mind of their own. I took a swig of my drink and damn near choked. Naomi and I sat there on the couch together, after Xen left. She came and got closer to me. I could see it in her eyes that she was starting to heat up.

"You wanna know something?" She asked.

"Only if you want to tell me."

"We actually had our eyes on you the moment we saw you. We wanted to see who would get to you first, but you didn't react or try to hit on us at all."

"So y'all made a bet on me huh?"

"No, not like that. I mean. . ."

"It's cool."

"No no. You see, I actually wanted to talk to you, because I think you're very intriguing. You're very mysterious."

"Is that right?"

"Yes."

She placed her drink down on the floor next to her and ran her hand along my inner thigh. Her hand was soft, warm and fluffy. They were marvelous hands. I wanted to see more of them wrapped around other parts of me. Suddenly, I you'd feel my blood rushing and boiling. My pole began to rise and grow harder. The whiskey was starting to do its job. I tilted my head back and down my drink, then placed the empty glass on the floor next to me. She undid my belt, unzipped and pulled down my pants. Then came the boxers. My pole swung out like a baseball bat and she caught it with those meaty hands of hers.

"OOH. IT'S SO BIG!"

She took a mouthful and went to work. The whiskey had kicked in even more. I begin thinking that everyone could hear us, from her loud moans and sound effects. She went on and on, using two hands at times. Spitting and stroking it slowly. The she got faster and faster. My legs and knees were about to fold and I knew that she could feel it. She looked up at me with those wicked eyes of hers, as if she was waiting for my arrival and sure enough I had arrived. She took it all, then swallowed every last drop. She got up, went into the bathroom, wash her mouth out, then told me that she was going to bed.

"You can sleep here tonight. There's a blanket in the closet there. Goodnight."

She smiled, then was off to her bedroom.

"What in the hell just happened?" I thought.

It was now four am and I was up still drinking. I couldn't sleep. I never could sleep whenever I stay over someone else's place. I had the lights off and was drinking in the dark. I sat there in silence, still in disbelief about what happened between Naomi and myself. A figure appeared in the darkness and walked towards the bathroom. I couldn't make out who it was. So I waited to see who would come out. I heard the sounds of the person pissing, then the toilet flushing. The door opened and the person was coming towards me.

"I see that you're still up. Mind if I join you?"

It was Xen.

"Not at all," I said.

She sat right next to me. I didn't have any pants on. Just a t-shirt and my boxers. She had on an oversized shirt and her hair was in a ponytail.

"So I take it you can't sleep either huh?" She asked.

"I can never sleep whenever I'm over someone else's and if I do, it's not for very long."

"Could you pour me some of that please?"

She went and got a glass. When she was on her way back, she looked just as good as when she walked into the bar last night.

"So what made you go down to the bar last night? You don't have a woman?"

"I just needed to get out and get some fresh air. Also, no. I do not have a woman."

"You're such an appealing young man. You arouse my curiosity. Naomi and I knew that from the moment we laid eyes on you. It's the reason why you're here right now. How do you feel about God, sex and death?"

"One is the greatest artist of all time. Another is something you do when you make time for it and can be overrated when abused. The other one is something that takes your time away."

"How come you're so good with words? I've never heard anyone, let alone a man speak this way. Are you a poet, writer or something?"

"I just spill my thoughts and emotions and let whatever at the time soak it up. Nothing too special."

"SEE! There you go again with the beautiful words! I'm not sure if you know this already, but Naomi and I wanted to have a threesome with you. I apologize for just throwing this on you."

"Although I'm very flattered, I don't think it would work. One of the three will not enjoy it as much as the other two."

"I think it would. Naomi and I have great chemistry and no jealousy, but I understand if you don't want to."

"It's not that. It's. . ."

"So would you fuck me then?"

She crossed her legs and sat back waiting for my response. She sucked at her drink, without taking her eyes off of me. I could feel her eyes piercing through my skin. It was those goddamn eyes and legs of hers. Even though all she had on that oversized shirt, it still made me want to take her. It left my mind to only imagine what could possibly be underneath. She uncrossed her legs and lifted up her shirt. My eyes raised and so did my dick. I could feel my soul trying to detach itself from me and go into her. Unlike Naomi, she came prepared. She had a game plan and was about to execute it. She was teasing me. I opened my legs and out of the side of my boxers came my dick.

"Oh sorry," I said.

"That's all right," she said.

She took a long swig of her drink.

"Can I touch your face?" She asked.

"Uh sure," I said.

She touched me with those long fingers and delicate hands of hers. I couldn't resist the temptation.

"I want to fuck you and I know that you want to fuck me, because I can sense it," she whispered softly in my ear.

Her hand moved down to my dick and popped him back out. She bent her head down to kiss him, then opened her mouth to take him in. I felt myself throbbing like my heart. My head went back and my eyes were closed.

"I'm going to ask you again. Will you fuck me?" She asked.

"Shit yes," I said.

We went round after round and woke up the sun, instead of it waking us up. We were so loud that I thought Naomi would hear us, but she must've been in a deep sleep, because she didn't come in there. That morning, Xen was my coffee and I was her breakfast.

I never saw them again after that. Though I went to the bar we had met at many more times after, but neither of them had shown their face. Naomi, I didn't mind seeing again, but Xen was a whole other beast. She had done to me what I had done to many other women. That was fuck my heart and left my mind curious. One night, a woman who looked identical to Xen had come over to my table. For a brief moment, I thought that she was Xen, pretending to be someone else.

"May I join you?" She asked.

She had a very heavy accent and relaxed shoulders. Her face was thin and her eyes were contagious. Her smile was smooth and her figure was handcrafted by God.

"Here we go again," I thought to myself.

The Lion, The Eagle and The Shark

There was Frank, who was about the break into the fashion world. He probably would have gone pro in baseball or basketball, but injuries took him out. He had a full thick beard and eyes that looked as if he smoked half of the day and slept the rest of it. No matter how chaotic things got, he always spoke in the same melancholy tone. His favorite thing to say was "I just be chillin'". To society, he was the guy who wasn't doing anything with his life, except for wearing cool clothes, but those who knew him knew the truth. The women would want to meet him, just to get closer to him. They wanted to see if he was as cool as his images and style portrayed him to be. Some went all out, but others only came for a moment. Though, all of them they got their answer, then left. He had been single for years afterwards and striking out with the women.

Then there was Nor. Nor was a smooth black muthafucka, who had a mouthpiece. I mean this cat could talk a woman out of her panties one minute, and the cops out of writing him a ticket the next. Nor was a funny muthafucka. He enjoyed music and sneakers. He knew about all of the sneakers before they even released. His skin was darker than the gums of a smoker. The thing about Nor was that he was good with the women, but could never get serious with any of them. Nor was the guy to see if you wanted to be ahead of the curve in sneakers. Why he was one of the first one's of my generation to bring notice to certain sneakers. People would ask him for his opinion often, when it came to sneakers. Hell I even think women even fucked him, just to get some information on a certain sneaker.

I was the last one to round it out. Now I wasn't as cool and fly as Frank or smooth, with many different sneakers as Nor. All I did was write books, fuck whenever the opportunity presented itself and carried depression around like a goddamn backpack. We were all just trying to make it in the world. Each of us coming from poor backgrounds and not having much. The little bit we did have, we would try to stretch it and place it into our passions. One night, New Years night to be exact. We went out into the night. The past year was hell for all of us and we just wanted to bring in the new year with some type of enjoyment. So we went downtown to the bars. Frank was the driver. Nor and myself were the ride alongs. We each wore our best attire and was ready to take on the night. I personally, was ready to get drunk. So I brought my own personal bottle of whiskey to drink on, while we were making our way on down there. Frank picked me up first.

"What's happenin' playa?" Asked Frank.

"Shit. Ready to get this night started," I replied.

I got in and we were off to pick up Nor. I looked down near his armrest and saw a bottle of Dusse.

"I see we were thinking just alike," I said.

I held up my bottle and he laughed. He cut on the music and we were in the zone. As we got closer the Nor's crib, the streets started to shake up the bottom of the car. It was like we were driving on rocks and stones. We made it to Nor's crib and waited. While we waited, I cracked open my bottle and took swigs of it. The warmth of the whiskey hit my throat and touched my stomach with heat. Nor came out and got into the car.

"HELL YEAH BRETHREN! It's time to dive into these streets, freaks and drinks."

He pulled out a bottle of Cognac. Frank and I looked at each other, then showed off our own bottles. Frank turned up the music again and we were off again.

We reached downtown and each took a shot of our own bottle. Then another and another one.

"Let's have a good night brethren."

We got out the car and walked into the night. The first bar we went into was full of smoke. The bartending service was rude and unaware. The women were in there, but the environment was tasteless. Frank and Nor had left to take another hit from their bottle. I stayed behind, thinking that I would get some service. After waiting around for about ten minutes to see if I would get service, I left. I saw a security guard standing at the door.

"I just would like to say that the bartending service here fucking sucks!"

I walked outside to head to the car, when I saw Frank and Nor inside of another bar to my left. I walked in and saw an old classmate of mine as well. She was dancing and wore a tight dress that showed off her curves. Frank and Nor were already at the bar drinking and talking to two women, who were both gorgeous and had the body of a goddess. Both has an ass that sat up right and could feed the homeless if it was eatable. I walked up to the bar and got myself a drink quicker than you could say hello. I stood excited and tipped the bartender a big chunk of dough. I looked around to see the everyone in the bar enjoying themselves. Women with fat asses and men who were drunk. I saw Frank and Nor rapping with the two women and smiled. It was a good sight to see my brethren being embraced. As the night went on, Frank had gotten the number of my old classmate and was on the verge of getting the shorty who looked as if she was meant to be in a fashion magazine or video. My eyes smiled. I turned my attention towards Nor and saw him and the other woman chatting it up, with huge smiles on their faces. Soon, the four of them came up to the bar and got four shots. Each of them threw their heads back and downed their drinks. The dj turned on a song that awaken the drunken souls. The two women stood at the bar, while Frank and Nor stood across from them. Each of them just looking at one another. I watched this go on for a few minutes, then pulled them toward each other. I pulled the shorter woman who had been talking with Nor onto him. They both smiled and begin dancing. I looked into their eyes and saw happiness, drunkness and light. Nor smile was so damn huge that he had the look of the joker. I started to pull the other woman on to Frank, when she said, "your friend doesn't want me".

I stood there in disbelief.

"Would you like to dance with me?" She asked.

"I can't, since you were already talking with my buddy."

I walked over to Frank and told him about this, then pulled him towards her.

They stood there talking, but didn't dance. Well, at least Nor was getting some action. I continued drinking. The more I drank the more I saw the demons inside of everyone around. We were all unleashing ourselves onto the night. The night went on and I sat at the bar drinking away. As I was about to leave, I couldn't find Nor or Frank. I saw the two women, but not my brethren.

"Did they leave you?" The shorter one asked.

"I believe so," I said.

"Aww. Would you like for me to take you home?"

"No thanks. I'll just call an Uber."

"Are you sure?"

"Certainly."

"Okay, well get home safely," she said.

I was about to call the Uber, when I thought about walking to where Frank had parked. So I did. When I got there, I could see Frank's car, with the driver door open.

"Shit! I hope no one had robbed them!"

I walked fast towards the car and open the door. I didn't see no wounds or nothing missing. I only saw two bodies, who each were slumped over drunk. Both looked as if they had fought alcohol and loss.

"Are y'all all right?" I asked.

Neither of them said anything.

"Frank, would you like for me to drive?" I asked.

"Huh?" He replied.

"Frank threw up in his seat and arm rest," uttered Nor.

"Would you like for me to drive?"

"Yeah," said Frank.

He got out of the car and climbed into the passenger seat. I got in the driver seat and had forgotten all about what Nor had said about Frank throwing up. Though, I had been drinking, I still had my wits about me. I called up a woman who I knew would be up and help me get through this. Just hearing her voice settled my mind. I got to Nor's place first.

"I'm here Nor."

"Huh?"

"I'm at your place."

"Okay, give me a second."

He opened the car door, but didn't get out. He sat there as if he was waiting on God to come and carry him inside the house.

"Nor you have the door open! You have to closed the door man. I understand we're in front of your house, but we still can get rob or killed."

Two minutes went by, before he finally got out and walked towards his front door. I waited to make sure he got in safely. After about three attempts, the front of his door opened and he was inside.

"Did Nor get inside safely?" Asked the young woman on the phone.

"Yeah he did. Now I'm on my way to drop off myself and Frank. AH SHIT! How can I do that, if Frank can't drive himself home?"

"Can you drop him off at his place, then drive back to yours and have him pick it up in the morning?"

"I'm not sure. Luckily, he parents lives close by me. Literally, on the next street. So I may just drop him and his car off in front of their place, instead of his. Then I'll just walk myself back home."

"Is that safe?"

"It'll be okay."

I arrived in front of Frank's parents place.

"Frank? Look man, I'm about to walk home. I'm leaving you here in front of your parents. Would you like for me to turn off the car or leave it on?"

I could tell that he was drunk. So drunk that he could barely open up his mouth.

"Leave it on," he said.

I let it running, then walked off. As I started walking, I felt bad, then turned around. I opened up the car door, then turned off the car. I started back walking away again, then the bad feelings came back. I stopped, turned back around and this time, walked up on the porch and knocked on the front door of his parents. I looked down at my watch and it was 3AM. I didn't want to do this, especially, at the time of night. Well, morning.

"Who is it?"

A soft spoken voice asked from the other side of the door.

"It's Sin. I meant Sinclair. I have Frank with me and I need your help."

"Hold on," said the softly spoken voice.

The door opened and it was his father and mother both standing there.

"Hey, sorry to disturb you, but I have Frank with me and he's drunk. I didn't want to leave him inside of the car, so I figured it would be best to come and get you all. I know it's late, but I didn't know what else to do."

"HE'S DRUNK? Frank don't drink," said his mother.

She walked on down and opened up the car.

"FRANK!"

"What y'all was drinking?" Asked his father.

"We each had our bottle," I said.

"Was he drinking that you're holding?"

"Nope."

"Are you drunk?"

"Not at all."

Frank and his mother was walking up onto the porch and into their home. He was leaning on her, while they both were walking by. I looked at Frank's face and his eyes were closed, but his face was stuck in a smile.

"Thank you, Sinclair. You need a ride home?" His dad asked.

"No thank you," I said.

I took my bottle of Jim Beam and walked home. As I was walking, my mind reflected on the night. The eagle, which was Frank, flew to the highest of the high tonight. The shark, which was Nor, swam deep into the ocean as he possibly could. The lion, which was myself, survived and was still on the prowl.

About the author:

Scottie Waves is a writer and poet, who grew up in Mobile, Alabama. He first encountered writing and poetry through trauma at the age of six, when he was raped by his babysitter. It was then, he had found a reason to live. Now living in Richmond, California, he has since then published numerous of books and continues to write to this day.

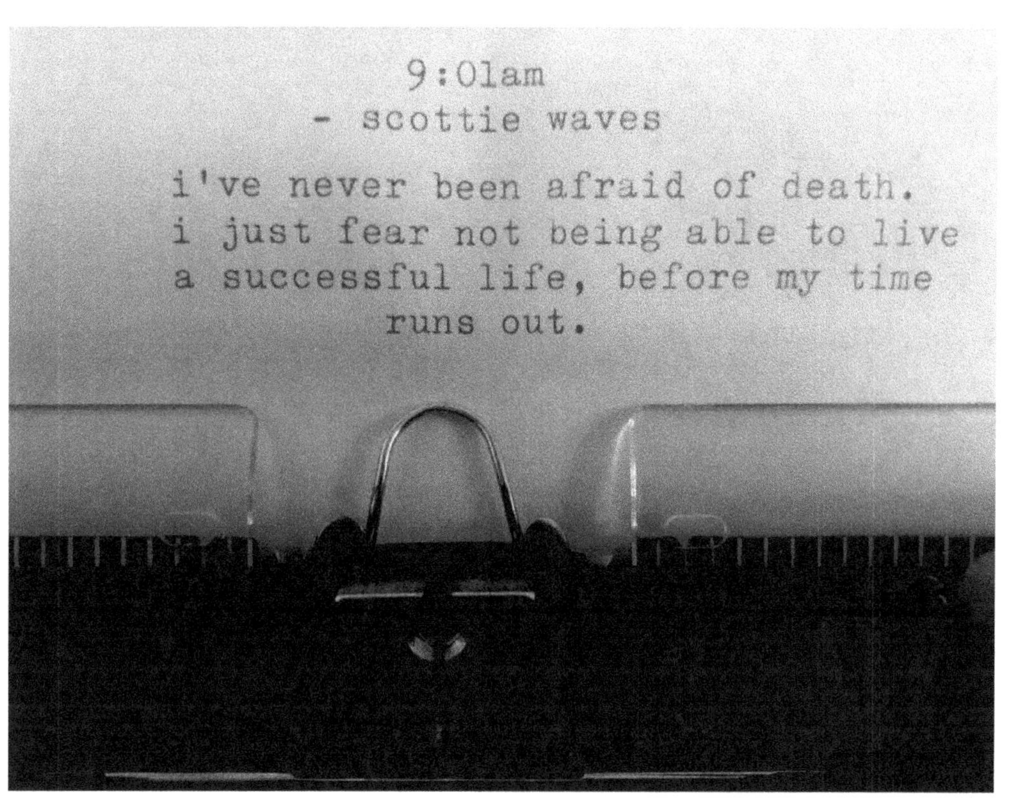

THANK YOU FOR READING.